Friend of My Enemy

A Medieval Fiction novel about an unlikely friendship in a dangerous land

Marina Pacheco

Marina Pacheco

There is a glossary and author's notes at the back of the book

CONTENTS

1. Chapter 1 — 1
2. Chapter 2 — 15
3. Chapter 3 — 25
4. Chapter 4 — 31
5. Chapter 5 — 39
6. Chapter 6 — 52
7. Chapter 7 — 66
8. Chapter 8 — 73
9. Chapter 9 — 88
10. Chapter 10 — 99
11. Chapter 11 — 109
12. Chapter 12 — 115
13. Chapter 13 — 132
14. Chapter 14 — 142
15. Chapter 15 — 149

16. Chapter 16 163

17. Chapter 17 168

18. Chapter 18 175

19. Chapter 19 182

20. Chapter 20 197

21. Glossary 209

22. Author's notes 211

Also By 213

About Author 218

Chapter 1

Vomit flooded Galen's gullet, filled his mouth, seared his nostrils and brought him to panicked consciousness. He coughed to clear his airways, gasping in air and trying to swallow the rest down. His head banged against the side of a horse and the smell of its sweat mingled with the acid at the back of his throat. He couldn't breathe, and not just because of the sick, but the position. He was folded over, his arms tied behind him and his feet bound.

'Help.'

He had intended it as a shout. It came out so softly that even Galen couldn't hear it over the pounding of the horses' hooves.

Everything was red. Was it blood or the setting sun? His head throbbed. No, not only his head, his whole body was in agony and his guts felt like they were on fire. Galen forced his eyes wide to clear the spots dancing about in his vision.

Where was Alcuin? Had the Moors taken him too? There were at least a dozen horsemen following the horse he was on. The one directly behind appeared to have a black bundle on its back that might have been Alcuin. Through the fractured haze of his vision, Galen couldn't make out any more than that. He doubted he could tell a head apart from a pair of feet right now.

'Please, dear God,' he prayed, 'keep Alcuin safe.'

But what did that mean? Was safe here, alive, or back at the ship? Terror of being all on his own filled Galen.

He immediately regretted that. Better if Alcuin had been left behind. But didn't he remember... Alcuin being tied up too, and the bishop? Were they the only ones to have been taken from the contingent that had sailed on the Wave Rider?

If they were, then why? Galen feared the answer would not be a good one. The Moors had their own religion, like the vikings. Would they be equally hostile to Christians?

The terror of his return to consciousness made Galen try to hang on and stay awake. He felt dreadful, nauseous and unable to move his body that was in such exquisite pain, even a torturer would marvel at it.

'Please God, save us all,' he said and, despite his best efforts, slipped back into oblivion.

Alcuin prayed Galen was suffering less than he was, but he doubted it. This ride, trussed up on the back of a horse, the sun burning through his black robes, was destined to go down in Alcuin's memory as one of the most painful he'd ever had to endure. He was face down and air got knocked out of him each time the horse's feet hit the ground. It pressed on his fractured ribs, causing an agonised haze to obscure his vision.

He dreaded to think what this ride was doing to Galen's injuries. He was in a bad enough way as it was. If he bled more heavily, there would be no saving him.

The party of Moors rode through the night without stopping. They would only push themselves in this way if they were being chased by an enemy, Alcuin realised. Would it be better for him and Galen if the enemy caught up with them or if they didn't?

On the second day, the pale clay path turned into a leaf-fringed blur and they seemed to be on a sustained uphill path. For hours now Alcuin seldom slipped forward to press against the rider. Most of the time he slid down to the less comfortable rump of the horse. The dust raised by all the horses' hooves increased his discomfort by making his throat rough and dry.

It was still light when the path turned into a cobbled road and the horses slowed from a trot to a walk. Alcuin was so exhausted he could no longer even press down with his elbows to raise his body and get the gap necessary to breathe. Thankfully, without the constant pounding, that was no longer necessary.

The cobbles reduced in size from wide slabs to a more consistent squarish block. The leaves vanished, replaced by whitewashed and stone walls. They were no longer in countryside but amongst houses. Feet gathered along the side of the road, but Alcuin didn't have the strength to look up and see the people properly.

There was chatter, though, and even the occasional shout of somebody hawking their wares. Funny how he couldn't understand a word, but he knew it was calling people to buy. As they continued riding, ever upwards,

Alcuin realised that they were in a really big town. One that easily rivalled Lundenburh in its size.

Wherever they were, it must surely mean this ordeal was over, but most likely another was about to begin. For all Alcuin had been praying for an end to his torment, he now wished to prolong it just a little longer.

That wasn't to be. The horses passed through a shadow that denoted a covering to the passage through the thickest stone wall Alcuin had ever seen, and the feet that had lined the street vanished. Now there was just the neat paving and the horses coming to a halt in what seemed to be a courtyard.

Alcuin's body was jostled as the rider of his horse dismounted. Then there was some chatter, the tired voices of men who'd ridden long and hard. Then feet approaching.

Somebody grabbed a handful of his robe by the neck and hoisted his head up. Alcuin took a great gasp of air. He was staring into the leering face of a swarthy man. The Moor grunted, as if noting that his load was still alive. Then he pulled at Alcuin like he was a sack of grain and dragged him off the horse.

Alcuin hit the ground hard. His bound hands and feet made it impossible to break his fall. He took a moment to catch his breath and subdue the fresh pains shooting through him before he rolled over.

In the seconds he lay on his back looking up, he was struck by how blue the cloudless sky was. Then he noted the high, impenetrable fortress walls and finally the swarm of black flies buzzing all about him.

A cry of disgust drew his eyes back to the men and he realised they were converging on one horse. No, on the black-robed load on the back of the horse. Holy Father, Alcuin thought, as a quiver of dread shot through him. Please, don't tell me he's dead.

The well-dressed young Moor, Hatim, who'd appeared to be the leader when they were taken hostage, burst out from amongst the men and stormed over to Alcuin. He looked taller than he had on the beach. His skin was dark, his beard was neat and trimmed to a point. He wore wide trousers tucked into his boots, and a tunic in a floral-patterned light linen, the top of which was obscured by leather armour. His head was covered by an iron helmet, the top of which came to a point, while wide bands of cloth cushioned the bottom.

'You,' he snapped in Latin as he grabbed Alcuin by his habit and dragged him over the cobbles to Galen. 'What devilment is this?'

Alcuin blinked back his own tears of pain and took a first anxious look up at the horse. A slick of blood covered Galen from the waist down and stained the flanks of the chestnut horse a deeper red.

'Dear God!' Alcuin would have crossed himself if his hands were free.

'What depraved acts have you people perpetrated on this little monk?' the Moor hissed. 'Was he a party to it? I've heard some vile things about you people with your vows of celibacy, but this goes beyond what Allah can endure.'

'What?' Alcuin was in a daze, uncertain he could believe his ears.

'You have been practising sodomy on this young monk, haven't you? Tell me, did he give his consent or did you force your attentions on him?'

'Me?' Alcuin said, aghast at the accusation. 'It wasn't me.'

'Who then? The bishop, was it him?' the Moor asked, pointing at the motionless bundle of the bishop, still secured to his horse.

'No, not the bishop either.'

'Don't lie to me!'

'Is he still alive?' Alcuin whispered, too battered and worried for Galen to have the strength for more.

'Only just.'

'Then will you take him down from there, please, and fetch a healer? I will tell you everything if you'll just do that.'

'You love him?' The Moor tilted his head as this new idea occurred to him.

'As a brother only. I assure you.' Alcuin prayed with every ounce of his being to God to save Galen because nobody else seemed to have any intention of doing so. 'Please, don't just leave him there, help him!'

The Moor apparently shouted some orders because what Alcuin took to be slaves in plain, pale, un-dyed, long, loose robes, came running out, lifted Galen off the horse and carried him away. The older Moor, with deep brown skin that contrasted with his long white beard, who appeared to be the leader, said something. It was incomprehensible to Alcuin, but his tone was sardonic and seemed to irritate the younger man, but not so much that they came to blows.

'You, come too,' the Moor said to Alcuin, and followed it with more orders in his own tongue to the rest of the retinue.

It must have been at his bidding that two of the horsemen grabbed Alcuin by an elbow of each of his still bound arms, undid the ties around his ankles and hoisted him to his feet. He was so wobbly that it was just as well they maintained their grip as they walked him into a building, the size of which Alcuin could hardly comprehend.

The closest he could come to understanding this massive structure was the legend of the hall of giants he'd heard as a boy. The giants carved their homes out of the peaks of the mountains. This was clearly built by men, stone by stone, but equally massive.

Alcuin was dragged through a towering doorway shaped like a giant's keyhole. It had straight walls on the lower half and a circular top painted in broad red and white stripes.

'Please,' he shouted after the Moor, trying to keep an eye on Galen in the gloomy interior, 'what are you going to do to my friend?'

'I will attempt to heal him,' Hatim said, with barely a backward glance.

'You?' Alcuin said, in increasing alarm. 'What can you do?'

The Moor gave an exasperated sigh.

'You sound just like an ignorant barbarian when you speak that way. At least my people respect and admire men of learning. I am the best doctor you will find in these parts. The great Abu al-Qasim taught me in Córdoba. I am my uncle's personal physician. Many at court and in the city would thank Allah for having me treat them. Your friend should be honoured that I am bothering to heal him.'

Alcuin had no wish to irritate the Moor, especially when his and Galen's situation was so precarious. So he said no more, there was no point. No reassurance from the Moor would have sufficed in any case.

How long would they walk before they reached their destination? They'd briefly emerged out of one large, cloistered building and were heading into another even larger and considerably brighter building. How many rooms would they have to traverse?

The slaves carrying Galen had vanished now. This section of the cloistered palace was quieter but he could still hear were the footsteps of the surrounding men, the clank of their weapons and the distant chirp of birds oblivious to the drama playing out in the halls of men. Further out was the laughter of children, the sound of a stringed musical instrument and the chatter of women. It had such an intensely domestic feeling that Alcuin's eyes stung with sudden tears. After all he'd been through, why did the sound of women and children upset him the most?

Finally he was pushed through yet another wide doorway and then pulled to a halt. For a moment Alcuin stood blinking, dazzled by bright light coming through an open doorway and two arched windows to either side. Then he gasped as he spotted Galen laid on a white marble table and being stripped of his clothes. The slaves worked efficiently so that soon his incredibly skinny, pale, naked body was all that remained.

Alcuin realised there was quite a gathering of people, two of whom moved to assist the others in repositioning Galen's body so that he was face down but with his behind propped up and facing the doorway. The Moor rapped out more instructions and another slave hurried forward and laid a bundle on the wooden table that stood beside the marble one where Galen lay.

The bundle turned out to be the sack with Galen's medical supplies, the one given to him so many months ago by Brother Benesing. The Moor tipped the contents of the sack onto the table and sorted through the vials and bundles of herbs. He uncorked one vial and sniffed the contents, and his expression grew thoughtful.

'You, monk, explain these things to me,' he said, pointing at the medicines.

'They are herbs to help Brother Galen.'

'In what way do they help?'

'I'm not entirely sure.' Not for the first time, Alcuin wished he knew more about medicine. 'Our Infirmarius gave them to me so that I could help Galen on our journey. I give him the herbs in a tea when he isn't feeling at his worst. I give him the syrup if he starts to bleed.'

'So he has been like this for a long time?'

'Years.'

'Barbaric,' Hatim murmured. 'What happened to him?'

'It's a long story. Could you at least untie me and let me sit down if you want it recounted?'

Hatim gave an order to the guard, and the man untied Alcuin and pushed him onto a low bench with a couple of wide cushions on it. Then he took up position beside Alcuin.

'I'm really in no condition to do any fighting.'

'Tell me about your friend,' Hatim said and sat opposite Alcuin on another low, cushion-covered bench on the opposite side of the room.

'What are you going to do to him?' Alcuin said, but avoided looking at Galen. He was lying so still and looked so pale that Alcuin feared what he'd see.

'I am going to attempt to heal him.'

'Oh no! I've had a leech working on Galen before and the man nearly killed him. I won't have you doing your weird foreign things to him. Just keep him still and give him the syrup and he'll recover.'

'In the same way as he recovered before?'

'Look, it may not be much, but at least he was alive.'

'Those circular burn marks all over his body, they were caused by your... leech?'

'The king's man, no less. He made Galen worse. Until his treatment, Galen was in a great deal of pain all the time, but after that butcher got hold of him, he was permanently cold as well.'

'He must be important for the king's leech to look after him.'

Alcuin immediately realised his mistake. At all costs, he couldn't let this Moor think Galen was important.

'Galen is a scribe and I'm an illuminator. We went to Lundenburh to produce a book of hours for the king, that is all.'

'So you are both men of learning?' Hatim said, and he appeared more interested than he had been up till then.

'Galen more than me. I can just draw. Galen can do translations and write poetry. He's the clever one.'

'So once again, I ask you, what happened to him to cause such a grievous injury?'

Alcuin sighed. He was obviously going to have to tell this insistent man what had happened. He wasn't sure if he should hurry through his tale so Galen could be treated quickly, or whether he should delay. No. Delay would only mean Galen's certain death. Maybe this Moor could do something like Madam Ivetta the first time they'd come across vikings. So Alcuin spoke about the rape in all the detail he'd been able to work out over the years.

'I see,' Hatim said at the end of the tale. 'Barbarous indeed.'

'Now that you know all about it, what are you going to do?'

'I am going to look inside your friend and see whether I can sew shut this injury which is so fragile it tears apart at the least provocation.'

'Look inside him?' Alcuin instantly regretted telling all. This man was even more barbarous than the leech, Irminric. 'No! It's impossible. It's flesh you're talking about. You can't sew flesh.'

'I assure you I can both do the investigating and the sewing. My teacher was a renowned surgeon, the greatest that has ever lived. Under his tutelage, and after it, I have sewn shut a wide variety of wounds and it has always worked remarkably well.'

'No!' Alcuin said and tried to jump up.

The guard slapped a powerful restraining arm on his shoulder and Hatim said, 'If you get in my way, I will have you sent straight to the dungeons and you won't know one way or another how your friend is doing.'

Alcuin bit his lip and gave an accepting nod.

'I'll give you no trouble.'

'Good, then I will begin,' Hatim said, but then walked out into the courtyard and shouted a name, apparently looking for somebody.

Alcuin heard him call Jariya a couple of times, but he had no idea whether that was somebody's name or some sort of order. Either way, a woman arrived, clutching a book to her chest, along with ink and a pen. Hatim said something in a voice tinged with exasperation, to which the woman returned a calm reply. Then the two came back into the room.

'My cousin,' Hatim said, waving a hand in the general direction of the woman, who remained behind him and slightly to his left. 'She will record everything I do here today.'

Alcuin was astonished that any woman was being allowed in a room with a naked man, but also that she was a record keeper.

But he was distracted from dwelling on the question as Hatim said, 'Shall we begin?' and picked up what looked like a fearsome metal implement, something to torture someone with, not help them.

'Shouldn't you rest first? I mean, you rode through the night,' Alcuin said, as a last desperate attempt to prevent this man from doing just as he pleased.

'Believe me, I would like nothing better than a good long bath and a rest, but if your friend is to survive, I must make haste.'

Alcuin clenched his fists and forced himself to sit still when every instinct screamed to leap up and rescue Galen. The only good thing he could see from this entire operation was that Galen was unconscious and wouldn't feel a thing.

Hatim inserted the slim metal implement into Galen's rectum and gently ratcheted it open. As he did so, Alcuin tensed, but there really was nothing he could do beyond working to keep his emotions under control.

'I can't blame you for looking alarmed,' Hatim said and looked up as a slave appeared holding a bowl of water with several cloths draped over his arm. Hatim washed his hands, then indicated for the bowl and cloths to be placed beside him on the marble table. 'But the situation is dire. So dire that I might never have attempted this operation but for the fact that I don't think this monk will live. He's lost far too much blood.'

'What?' Alcuin felt as if he'd been delivered a hammer blow with that news. So Galen was nothing but a plaything to this Moor. He had never intended to heal him after all. 'Galen has survived more than you can imagine.'

'Let us hope he will survive this too,' Hatim said, his full attention now on the task at hand. 'He is a challenge and something I have never attempted before. I'm curious to see how I do. My first impression isn't a good one. It's difficult to see exactly what is going on through all the blood.'

He spoke in a distracted way, all his attention focused on his task. Alcuin gripped his hands together so hard his fingers dug into his flesh. He was certain this urbane-looking man who worked with such deliberation had to be insane. He could barely watch as the Moor took a curved needle, threaded it with a black twine and started to sew inside Galen.

'God's tears!' Alcuin cried and jumped up. 'What are you doing?'

The guard pushed him back down and glowered at him.

'Don't distract me, this is extremely delicate work.' Hatim said, without looking up. 'Your friend has several tears in the lining of his rectum and I am trying to sew them together. It's tricky, for there is a mass of scar tissue that has developed over the years.'

'You're going to kill him.'

'On the contrary, I am trying to save his life. If I don't sew these wounds closed, he will bleed to death. For as you can see, it hasn't stopped yet.'

And so the Moor worked slowly and methodically, talking in his incomprehensible tongue as he did. His cousin listened intently and noted down everything he said in her book. On any other day, this whole dreadful scene might have fascinated Alcuin. Today, it was a vision of hell.

Chapter 2

Galen was at the bottom of a well, swallowed up by dark water. He had to work his way up to the inky blues and algal greens and up some more to the tiny yellow dot. But his arms and legs felt as though they were filled with lead and impossible to move.

Yet somehow that yellow dot got brighter and wider. He was floating, despite the weight of his limbs. Up some more and now there was just the brighter glow and white bobbing spheres tracing across his vision.

Galen opened his eyes. Not for the first time, he was certain of that. There was a familiarity to the space and yet at the same time, he had never seen anything like it.

He was staring up into an eight-sided star, high in a bright ceiling. The star was recessed and must have been open to the sky on the sides because light streamed in all around it, illuminating the repeating green, orange and blue patterns within the star and on the ceiling beyond. It glistened and shone as if it was slick with water. It was a mystery Galen was yet to fathom.

He might be awake, but he was far from alert, and the heaviness of his body pressed him into some sort of bench, although his head had a cushion to support it. He was also covered by a blanket whose smoothness was unfamiliar. At least he wasn't cold. It had been months since he could say that.

A creak drew his attention and, with a great deal of effort, he turned his head. A dark brown carved door had opened and a pair of pale-robed men carrying trays stepped inside and flanked the door. A taller, regal, dark-haired man entered, followed by two women and another man who was tall, slim, and so fair he looked like an angel although he had both a dagger and a sword tucked into his broad belt.

Women always drew Galen's attention and these two were especially surprising. They were on the short side with dusky skin, the shorter one darker than the other, but both darker than any women Galen had ever seen. The short one wore a long sea-green tunic made from silk, the other was dressed in a deep pink floral. Peeping out from the bottom of the tunics were voluminous striped silk trousers gathered at the ankles, while their feet were clad in patterned leather slippers. Blue for the smaller woman, red for the taller one. Long, sheer veils that trailed all the way to the floor covered their black hair and were held in place by bands around the head. The taller of the two, the one in the pink tunic, had a fringe of pearl beads on her scarf that swung back and forth as she walked.

The woman in the green tunic was carrying a musical instrument similar to a lute that she waved about as she spoke to the man. She sounded as if she was pleading, but playfully, with a smile tweaking the corners of her mouth. The other woman looked unamused, maybe even annoyed, and was clutching a large book to her chest, a pen gripped in her right hand.

'Ah, I see you are awake.'

The regal man was also dressed in silks: a long tunic in green, maroon and white stripes. Unlike the women whose tunics hung loose, the man's was tied at the waist with a broad band of heavy green silk and he sported the same puffy trousers, along with dark brown slippers.

That wasn't what held Galen's fascinated gaze. The man had outlined his blue-grey eyes with thick black makeup. Large pearls dangled from his earrings, a fringe of dark brown hair framed his face and fell to below his shoulders at the back and he smelled strongly of frankincense.

'Who?' Galen whispered, but again with the sense that he'd seen this man before and even asked the same question before.

'You're still not all with it, are you?' the Moor said, but a slight smile lessened the harshness of his words. 'I'm Hatim al-Qurtubi. My uncle, Zayd al-Ifriqi, is the amir of this place and I'm his heir. I took you from the beach where you were shipwrecked. You are now in my uncle's palace in Halab. Aside from being one of the most important men in the region, I'm also your doctor. I hope you realise what an honour that is. As proof of my expertise, you are still alive, contrary to expectations. I'm pleased with the way you are improving.'

'Oh.'

Galen's mind moved as slowly as mud, which was only good in that it was too slow to induce fear. Although, he was aware he was in a great deal of danger and, worse, surrounded by strangers.

'Brother Alcuin?'

'The other monk? He's fine.'

It seemed to Galen that much was left unsaid, but he didn't dare enquire further. It was good enough for now to know that Alcuin was still alive. He would worry about the rest later.

'You don't remember talking about this before, do you?'

'No,' Galen said and turned towards the woman in the pink dress.

She nodded to one of the slaves who put down the tray he'd been carrying and poured a reddish-coloured liquid from a pot with a long-necked spout into a small crystal cup that he handed to the woman.

'Drink,' Hatim said.

The two slaves came forward and lifted Galen so that the woman could hold the cup to his lips. An intensely sweet and bitter smell tickled his nose. Galen might have turned away, but the woman was too quick and tipped the contents into his mouth. He had no choice but to swallow, but he couldn't prevent a gag reaction and a cough.

'Don't resist,' Hatim said. 'That's tea with medicinal herbs and honey. It will aid your healing and give some much needed nourishment to your body. You are dangerously thin.'

Since everybody told him that, Galen just nodded. There wasn't anything he could do, anyway. The constant pain he lived with robbed him of his appetite. Now the tea sat like an acrid ball in his stomach.

His memory flew back to the time he'd first arrived in Yarmwick, battered and disowned and surrounded by disapproving strangers. The difference was that there he'd understood the language, and the buildings had a familiarity too. The abbey was also a place of cool, deep shadows under a frequently dark grey sky. Here the light had an intensity he'd never experienced before. It was so bright it hurt his eyes.

Now he longed to be back at the Abbey of Yarmwick with Alcuin and his fellow scribes. He was lost in this unfamiliar place. It seemed every day took him further and further from home.

He wished he had the strength to roll onto his side and pull himself into a ball, but he couldn't. Lying on his back, helpless, left him feeling vulnerable. He wanted to hide, to at least curl up on his side and pull the blankets over his head. It was foolish, like a child who thought he was safe from monsters if he couldn't see them.

'You appear to have improved,' Hatim said, 'so today we will bathe you.'

'What?' Galen's eyes flashed open again. 'A bath?'

'My cousins A'isha and Jariya will supervise.'

Hatim gave a nod to the women, who proceeded to issue a series of commands to the slaves who'd been standing to the sides, waiting. The two men converged on Galen, whipped his covering away, hoisted him into the air and deposited his now naked body face down on the cold marble surface of a large table.

'No.'

Galen was thankful that his position protected some of his modesty because he was all too aware of the women. The taller one in the pink dress now opened her book and took notes, as if what she was witnessing was an everyday occurrence.

Galen shuddered as, his face squashed sideways onto the table, he watched the slaves approach. Each was armed with a basin of water, a long, tan, fibrous-looking object and several cloths.

They dipped the fibrous object into the water and the thing came out bloated and dripping. Then the slaves slammed the coarse objects against his body and started scrubbing. They scraped away layers of skin and worked till Galen was rubbed raw. Maybe this was some form of torture? Although that would be accompanied by questioning, wouldn't it?

'No!' Galen gasped. 'Please, stop.'

'They won't stop until you are clean.' Hatim strolled to the head of the table so that he was within Galen's line of sight. 'They've been itching to do this. One of the worst things about you infidel is your lack of hygiene. Jariya even wanted to burn all your clothes.'

'What?' Galen gasped, horrified that they might have burned his cloak, the one and only gift his father had ever given him. 'No please, I beg of you, don't burn my clothes.'

'It's alright, I forbade that. She's made do with having everything pounded with soap and water for an hour by the slaves before she was satisfied they were clean.'

'Thank God.'

'We can say the same about you,' the Moor carried on, either oblivious to or unconcerned by Galen's distress. 'Your skin is filthy. It looks like you haven't had a wash in years. You're dirty all the way to your fingertips. Why are they black, by the way?'

'Ink, it's ink.' Galen screwed his eyes tight shut but couldn't prevent the tears that squeezed out between his lids. 'I'm a scribe.'

'Why are you so distraught?' Hatim's voice was right beside Galen's ear. 'Your body is tensed to breaking point. It will only cause you harm. You need to relax.'

Galen was too caught up in his world of humiliation and pain to register what the Moor was saying, but he sensed some response was needed so he nodded.

'Should I tell my cousins to be more careful?'

Without waiting for a response, Hatim said something to the women in his own language. But they snapped something back that sounded impatient, which made Galen lose hope that they might stop the torture.

'Are you unaccustomed to being bathed?' Hatim asked, back to speaking into Galen's ear. 'My cousins think that's why you are crying.'

As he spoke, a slave rolled Galen over, lifted his leg and began to wash thoroughly between his buttocks. Galen shuddered and gave a horrified moan but remained rigid and immobile.

'Fascinating. You are obviously appalled by your treatment, yet you do nothing to stave it off.'

Again, all Galen could do was nod. Nobody ever listened to him anyway, and the Moor was the least likely to do so.

'They are doing it on my orders,' Hatim said. 'Your injury is healing well, but I must monitor it. Until now I have been checking the colour of the exudate. At first it was mainly blood, but I'm happy to report that it is clearing and seems to be free of infection, so today I am going to examine the stitches.'

'What?'

Galen forced his eyes open, uncertain that the man was speaking Latin, for he made so little sense. Hatim held up an ominous tapered metal implement.

'I'm going to roll you over and examine you inside.'

Galen's eyes widened in horror and he whispered, 'No, please... don't.'

'It will be quite painless, I assure you,' Hatim said as he nodded for the slaves to roll Galen back onto his belly.

A spasm of terror shook Galen. This man brought back memories of the rape and his helplessness when Septimus seized him. He moaned in pain that was both physical and ripped through his heart as his body went rigid.

'This will be a lot easier if you don't clench all your muscles,' Hatim said as he pushed the cold metal speculum into Galen's anus.

Galen gasped, clutched his arms about himself and tried hard not to cry. There was no point. This Moor was going to do as he pleased, but he could not suppress his tears nor his shuddering breaths as the man probed him.

'That's looking much better,' Hatim said as he removed the speculum.

Galen pulled his legs towards his belly and tried to get his sobs under control as Hatim moved back to watching Galen's face.

'Are you in pain?'

Galen shook his head but shut his eyes tight. It was all he could do.

'Listen, I'm trying to help you, but I can't if you don't tell me the truth. So please, does it hurt?'

'No, I'm fine.'

'Oh, you're fine, are you?' Now Hatim sounded irritated. 'Well, if you are so healthy, why don't you get up right now and walk around the room?'

Galen opened his eyes, saw the look of anger on the Moor's face and tried to push himself up, determined to walk if it would keep him from further torture. But his illness robbed him of all strength. Dazzling points of light danced before his eyes and he was struggling even to rise.

'Oh, for the love of Allah, stop that right now!' Hatim snapped as he pushed Galen back down. 'You know, for somebody named after a great Roman healer, you have very little good sense.'

Galen gazed blankly at him, relieved he didn't have to walk. But he feared it would mean the entourage would return to wash him and stare at his naked body as if he was some freakish form of entertainment. No doubt the man would also continue to probe him with his wicked implements, and that made him feel sick all over again.

'Go back to sleep now,' Hatim said in an impatient tone that was all too familiar.

Galen had grown up dreading the annoyance of his father and the warriors of his father's hall. He'd met more exasperation and whispers of disgust at the Abbey of Yarmwick. Now there was this Moor who treated him as a plaything or experiment, but was equally dismissive.

Rough hands took hold of Galen again. He opened his eyes to discover that the two slaves were carrying him back to the bench-like bed.

Hatim himself flicked a blanket over Galen.

'Sleep now.' He looked like he was going to stomp out of the room. But then he stopped and turned back to examine Galen.

'You are a frustrating man! And you make me disappointed in myself. My teacher, Abu al-Qasim, encouraged his students to take an interest in their patients. To care not only for their physical well-being but for their state of mind and to heal the one and reassure the other.

'But with you,' Hatim said, pointing an accusing finger at Galen, 'you improve physically, which both surprises and pleases me, but your obvious distress is not allayed even though I am unfailingly polite. On top of that, I have my cousins tending to you and yet you still tremble and cry.'

Galen was aghast at the diatribe. An apology was surely not going to be sufficient. He wasn't even sure he understood what the man was saying. Right now, all he wished for was oblivion to reclaim him. Fortunately, the Moor solved the dilemma by giving an impatient tut and storming out of the room.

Chapter 3

'Eat, your Grace,' Alcuin said, kneeling beside the bishop and holding the food up to the old man's mouth which was barely visible by the light of a single flickering torch.

Sigburt lay half propped up on a stone ledge carved out of the wall and nibbled on his bread. His age meant he was slower to recover from their ride, which worried Alcuin. He placed the back of his hand against the bishop's forehead. It was still warm. He had a fever, but it seemed to be abating for he was sweating less.

'I'm fine,' Sigburt said and batted Alcuin's hand away.

At least he was back to being tetchy. It was worse when he'd been entirely willing to be looked after.

This led Alcuin to worry about Galen. It felt like ages since he'd witnessed the operation. When he'd been led away, Galen was wrapped in a blanket but left on the operating table. He prayed Galen was still alive. Surely the Moor would have told him if he'd died.

Or would he? Alcuin was hardly an honoured guest. He'd only witnessed Galen's operation because the Moor needed information on Galen's condition. A condition the Moor himself had described as precarious.

After that, the guards had led him out of the palace, across a wide courtyard and through a warren of buildings that looked to house the less illustrious members of the palace: the slaves, servants and soldiers. By this point, Alcuin was so exhausted he could scarcely take anything in as he'd staggered through the maze and out to another wide open, more dreary space.

He'd been walked to a hole in the ground guarded by two men. As they arrived, another group brought a man clothed in rags up to the same hole. The guards tied a rope around his waist, ignoring his pitiful cries and hands clasped together in supplication, and lowered him into the hole.

Alcuin looked down into the depths, horrified to see that it widened into a deep, rough-hewn cave filled with men. He feared he was to be lowered into that dreadful place, too. But the men accompanying him seemed to have stopped only to pass the time of day with the other guards. After a brief exchange, they poked Alcuin to get him into motion and led him to a barred entrance in a squat, red stone building.

The shriek of the gate sent a shiver through Alcuin, as did the stairs that led down into blackness. Alcuin started counting but lost his place somewhere after a hundred as they went down and down until the daylight vanished and they only had torches to light the way. At the bottom was a circular hall surrounded by barred cells. If there were other occupants in the cells, he couldn't tell.

They shoved him into one on the right and he discovered that the bishop was already there, a hunched up bundle, shivering in the corner. It had taken all the strength remaining to Alcuin to get the bishop lying down on the single stone shelf in the room before he'd curled into a ball and also given himself up to oblivion.

Alcuin had no idea how long ago that had been, without the light of the sun to give him an idea of time passing. All he could do was make a mark on the wall each time food was brought. He suspected it was once a day. It felt long enough, sitting in the dark, waiting for the measly stale loaf and single jug of water.

He dipped the bread into the water and fed some more to the bishop. Alcuin was surprised that the bread was edible. At least it wasn't mouldy, even if it was hard as a rock. The water was also clean and sweeter than he was used to. He feared what diseases they might take from drinking water instead of beer, but so far neither he nor the bishop had suffered any ill effects.

The sound of footsteps drew his attention from the bishop. Since they'd only just got their food there was no reason for the guards to return. A pair of soldiers blocked the flickering light, one of whom motioned for Alcuin to stand aside.

He did as ordered, but fear filled his heart. He'd been wondering when they'd be called again. There had to be a reason he and the bishop were in a cell rather than being dumped into the pit.

'Take your filthy hands off me,' the bishop said and slapped away the guard who reached for him.

'Your Grace, it might be best just to go along with–' Alcuin stopped as the guard slapped the bishop so hard across the mouth that his head snapped backwards.

Then they grabbed the bishop by his robe and dragged him from the cell and up the stairs. Alcuin made the sign of the cross several times as he sent a continuous string of prayers up to heaven, begging for divine intervention for himself, Galen and the bishop. The quiet time they'd spent in the cells, dreadful as the darkness was, seemed better than whatever unknown thing awaited them outside.

Alcuin lowered himself back onto his knees and continued his prayers. It was the only thing he had left to him. But it was difficult to focus.

Would he see the bishop or Galen again? What did the Moors intend to do with them? He'd assumed they'd been taken for ransom at first, for why else bother taking them at all?

If the Moors were offended by their religion they would most likely just have killed them. Unless they intended to make a spectacle of the killing as a lesson to other people. Alcuin had heard there were Christians in this Moorish caliphate, so that was one possibility.

But if they weren't taken for either of those purposes, then why? Slavery was another option, but a more probable fate for the fit and healthy sailors. Why take an old man and a frail one such as Galen?

Which brought his thoughts full circle back to worrying about Galen and whether he was still alive. If he was, Alcuin worried even more. Galen would be struggling without him. To be surrounded by strangers who meant him no harm was hard enough for Galen. To be surrounded by enemies must be a hundred times worse.

It felt like an age before Alcuin heard the shriek of the gate far above. There was the sound of footsteps and the bishop was tossed into the cell. He landed heavily on the floor and didn't move.

'Your Grace,' Alcuin cried, as he scrambled across to him.

His hand touched the bishop's back and came away wet and sticky.

'They beat me, boy!' the bishop gasped. 'Those damned Moors whipped me.'

Alcuin could understand his rage, but it was a futile emotion. The Moors would hardly care about the rank and status of an Anglo-Saxon bishop. On the contrary, it would make them a target in this land where they worshipped a different God.

It was a terrifying thought. He wanted to curse the old man who had forced him and Galen to leave the safety of their abbey and tipped them into so much danger.

'I was hoping they'd taken you to hold for ransom. The Moors must know how much bishops are worth.'

'I offered them as much.' Sigburt pushed himself up onto his knees, his hands still flat on the floor. Alcuin hurried to assist him the rest of the way onto his feet and then supported him onto the bench. 'But they aren't interested in a ransom.'

'What do they want?'

Alcuin's fear grew because it sounded like the Moors were similar to the pagan vikings who took ordinary people as slaves but tortured any monks and nuns they came upon.

'They want my second treasure.'

There was an odd note of defiance mixed with amusement in the bishop's voice.

'What is the second treasure, Your Grace?' This was the answer to Alcuin's riddle. The Moors were after something greater than a ransom.

'Best you don't know,' Sigburt said, patting Alcuin's arm as he held the old man upright. 'Now help me lie down. On my side, my back is aflame. I will hold out as long as I can, Brother Alcuin, and buy you some time. Your duty is to escape, you and Galen both.'

'Yes, Your Grace.'

'Beware of the Moors, for it is not just your body that is in peril,' Sigburt mumbled. 'They will try to turn you to their religion. Galen won't turn, I know that for certain, but you must resist their temptations too, Brother Alcuin.'

The bishop's low opinion of him shocked Alcuin almost as much as the realisation that martyrdom wasn't the only risk in a kingdom that was antithetical to his faith. It made escape all the more imperative, but he couldn't see how. They were underground. The solid bars of their cell showed no signs of decay. The stone walls also didn't lose a single grain when he tried to dig into them. And if he got out, how was he supposed to find Galen? Assuming he was still alive.

Chapter 4

Galen lay in bed trying to ignore the slow throbbing pain in his guts. He would have liked to move position for his shoulder blades and hips were digging into the bench, but he didn't have the strength to do it.

The warm glow of the sun through his lids made everything red. Since he'd arrived in this strange place, he'd learned to keep his eyes shut upon waking so that the Moors didn't realise he was conscious. The moment they noticed he was awake, the women and slaves would descend to clean him and then force some liquid down his throat.

It wasn't that he refused to drink. He would have, given half a chance to do it for himself. But they just swooped down and tipped a variety of liquids into his mouth.

At first it had just been the tea with herbs and honey. Lately, they also gave him a thin broth. He preferred the broth for its saltiness. It had an unusual flavour, but at least it wasn't unpleasant.

Nothing tasted familiar in this place and that reminded him of how far from home and alone he was. Strangers surrounded and manhandled him, ignored his pleas and spoke in a harsh guttural tongue he couldn't understand.

Worst of all, he had no idea what had happened to Alcuin. Was he still alive? Galen prayed he was, and that he was being treated well. Going on his own treatment, he wasn't so certain.

Every morning, the Moor, Hatim, noted his temperature, took his pulse, asked about his level of pain and checked how strong he was growing. Galen felt like he was something to be tested and then possibly discarded. Was Hatim using Alcuin for another such experiment? The very idea made Galen feel sick.

His mind was so sluggish, too. He couldn't work out what to do. No, that was self-deception. For most of his life he hadn't been a free agent. He'd felt trapped by his weak personality which made it difficult to rebel.

But really, none of those places, his father's burh, the abbey or the king's hall, had been prisons. Difficult, yes, but he could have walked out if he'd wished to. This place was different.

Here, he had to submit to the Moor. He had no physical strength to do anything else, even sitting upright was a struggle. For now, he had to watch and wait and pray that Alcuin would come to the rescue again.

Galen heard the door open and couldn't prevent a catch in his throat. There was a soft thud, followed by the sound of rustling clothes nearby.

'Are you going to open your eyes?'

It had to be Hatim. It seemed he was the only one in this place that could speak Latin. Galen, who had never been good at deception or at ignoring instructions, opened his eyes.

The room was becoming more familiar. Aside from the star on the ceiling there was the arched doorway that led into a courtyard. The glare from outside made it difficult to see more than an impression of white marble and dark green plants.

The arch leading to the courtyard was a complex structure where three sets of thin columns supported a white stone carved in such detail it looked like filigree work. Galen had never seen such ornate stone carving, nor so much of it. It was beautiful but overwhelming.

Today he paid it less heed because Hatim's slaves hoisted him up and pushed a cushion under his body. Now he was half upright and facing a gold cross on the edge of the marble table. It was a foot high and everything about it proclaimed home. From the large central gold boss decorated with knotwork, to the bejewelled arms. It was an Anglo-Saxon masterpiece.

'Oh,' Galen sighed.

'It's a fine piece of work,' Hatim said as he sat down cross-legged on a chunky embroidered cushion on the floor beside Galen's bed. 'I believe all those interwoven spiralling patterns are a distinctive feature of the work that comes from your land, not so?'

Galen glanced down at him, trying to understand what this was about. Up till now, the man had done nothing but examine his body and supervise everyone else who worked on him.

'Did you get it from the bishop?'

Galen doubted the wisdom of initiating a conversation. All the same, curiosity sometimes made him speak when it would have been wiser to keep his mouth shut.

'It's beautiful,' Hatim said. 'A beautiful rendition of an implement of torture. It is also a symbol of a religion with many similarities to my own, but is doggedly resistant to the words of our prophet. It has given my uncle quite a dilemma.'

'It has?'

Galen feared they expected him to give an answer to something, and he had no idea whether what he said would be accepted, or was even prudent to voice.

'On the one hand, my uncle should not allow this graven icon to exist. On the other, it would be a crime to destroy such a thing of beauty.'

Galen gazed at Hatim and held his breath. He too thought it would be a sin to destroy the cross, but not just because of its beauty.

'Your bishop compounds my uncle's dilemma.'

'Does he?' This conversation was growing more dangerous by the minute. 'I don't understand. Why did you even take us prisoners? How did we land up here?'

'By coincidence,' Hatim said with a laugh. 'My uncle goes on periodic raids into the kingdom to our north. During one of those raids, we came upon a group of shipwrecked vikings who, in exchange for their lives, told us they were chasing a boat carrying two great treasures. So we did some scouting, found you and took you with us. Now, we don't know what to do with you, and your bishop is being very stubborn about telling us where the second treasure is.'

'So the cross,' Galen said, pointing up at it, 'that is the first treasure?'

'Didn't you know that?'

'When we arrived at the boat, the treasures were already in the chest. The crew mentioned a cross, but we never saw it and neither Alcuin nor I knew anything about the rest.'

'So you only know of one treasure?'

Galen hesitated. Should he lie and say there was only one? No, he couldn't do that. He never felt comfortable lying and it showed on his face and gave him away.

'We also heard there were two treasures but we knew nothing about the other one. Was the second treasure not in the chest?'

'Not unless the second treasure is a load of silver coins.'

'I see.'

'You don't think that the money is a treasure either, do you?'

'Well… the bishop was determined to make a great impression on the pope. Money of any sort is hardly likely to do that.'

'Huh, it is as I suspected. My uncle is of the same mind, especially as the bishop won't tell us about the second treasure no matter how much he is tortured.'

'He is being tortured?' Galen was unable to suppress the jolt his body got at that. He'd started to relax because a mystery always diverted him, but at the mention of torture he was back to dread. 'And Alcuin?'

Hatim waved his hand vaguely, which Galen couldn't interpret but hoped indicated Alcuin was alright. Hatim's face, though, pulled into a deep thoughtful scowl.

'It didn't appear that there was anything of value left on the boat. We've gone through yours and the bishop's clothes. It was a disgusting experience. Your clothes were alive with vermin of every type. Do you not even notice all the creatures you carry with you?'

Hatim sounded exasperated but, thankfully, didn't pause long enough to get a response.

'I believe that is why you people are more sickly than we are and why you succumb to illnesses that merely incapacitate us for a while.'

Galen blinked, trying to keep his wits about him and focus on the dilemma of the treasure. If they found the second treasure would the Moors release them? Or at least, would they stop torturing the bishop?

'Maybe the treasure was lost overboard.'

'Why doesn't the bishop just say so if that's the case? Why does he continue to suffer? If this goes on much longer, my uncle really will keep to his threat and chop the man's hand off.'

'No!' Galen gasped.

Hatim shrugged.

'What can I do? Although I have already pointed out to my uncle that anyone who worships a God who was tortured to death is going to have a different attitude to torture than we are. I have a feeling my uncle could kill the bishop very, very slowly and he will still tell him nothing.'

All this talk of torture and death left Galen dizzy with panic, and he closed his eyes to gather his thoughts. What was the point of saying anything, anyway? He had no influence.

Still, there were things he had to know, so he screwed up his courage and asked, 'Could you tell me, please, exactly where I am?'

Hatim blinked in apparent astonishment at the question and said, 'Don't you know? You're in the town of Halab, in Al-Andalus. More specifically, we are in the Upper March that borders the Kingdom of Navarre in the foothills of the Pyrenees mountains.'

'The land of the Moors,' Galen murmured.

'Do you not know much about us?' Hatim said, and sounded surprised.

'Do you know much about Engla-lond?'

Hatim gave an exaggerated shrug and a slight smile. 'Your land is famous for its wool. Aside from that, I confess I know little. My focus has always been on the Dar al-Islam, the lands of the people who share the same faith and with whom we trade. They are to the south and east from Sudan all the way across to India.'

'I confess, I know more about Christendom, its people from kings to popes and saints, than I do of anything beyond that,' Galen said while he searched his memories for any information on the Moors and their caliphates. 'You have a different faith.'

'No, my friend,' Hatim said and shifted enthusiastically forward on his cushion, 'We are all peoples of the book who worship the same God. But your religion thinks that Jesus was the son of God, while we venerate Him as a prophet. The final and greatest prophet was Mohammed, peace be upon him, who gave us the definitive words of Allah, the most holy God. It is the mistake of all Christians that they fail to recognise him.'

This was all news to Galen, who had never spent much time considering other religions, possibly because he'd never come across a member of a different faith. He knew of the Jews, of course, and was aware that they engaged in trade across the known world. There were probably even Jewish traders in Lundenburh, but he'd never met them.

'Jesus is just a prophet to you?' Galen said, seizing on this one startling difference.

'Of course. There is no God but God. He is indivisible. If you set up a son and a spirit, you enter the realm of pantheism.'

While Galen was familiar with the fierce debates within Christendom that revolved around the topic, and the relationship Jesus had with God, he'd not come across a theology that relegated Jesus to mere prophet status. He didn't know what to think. Nor would it be wise to enter into debate with Hatim on the subject. It wasn't in his nature, even when he was among fellow monks. It was bound to be even more dangerous in this situation.

But Hatim was watching him with eyes that sparked with amusement and challenge. He'd not be easy to distract from what could easily turn into an interrogation. Then a sound drifted in, carried on the slight cool breeze of morning. It was a musical call, like an announcement. Over the last few days Galen had realised that they proclaimed this same announcement at regular intervals across the day, and that it was the same words, shouted by more than one man at every instance.

'Ah, the call to prayer,' Hatim said, springing to his feet. 'I must go, but we should continue this conversation on another day.'

His words caused a pang to pass through Galen. Prayer comforted him, soothed his mind and helped him concentrate, so he'd been praying regularly. But to be reminded of communal prayer made him miss Yarmwick and his fellow monks which, in turn, made his longing and fear for Alcuin grow.

Chapter 5

Alcuin paced the empty cell like a caged bear, waiting. This was what his life had become: a long, shadowy existence where hardly anything happened. What little occurred filled him with dread and wore away at his nerves. The bishop was being tortured, Galen might already be dead, and he could be next.

Even though he had no fondness for the bishop, they were in the same mess. His misfortune could quickly become Alcuin's. He wondered why Sigburt was being so stubborn about the second treasure. Why hadn't he denied its existence or said they had lost it at sea? Why did a man who looked to his own comfort and convenience ahead of everybody else's, endure torture for the mere sake of a treasure? It made no sense.

The shriek of the gate above made Alcuin jump and he hurried to peer through the bars of his cell. There was an interminable wait accompanied by the sound of boots thumping their way downstairs. Finally, there was a flare of light as a pair of guards stepped into the hall with Bishop Sigburt between them. The cell door was opened and they pushed the bishop through.

Alcuin hurried to support the old man as he staggered forward and guided him to the low stone bench. Alcuin's gaze flicked unwillingly to the man's hands and he gagged as he saw blood, a darker shade amongst dark shadows, seeping between the fingers of his right hand that he had clasped about the left.

'They cut off my finger, boy,' Sigburt rasped.

'You should just give them what they want, Your Grace,' Alcuin said as he helped the old man lie down.

'Never!' Sigburt said, and his eyes burned with passion.

'They'll kill you if you don't. They'll chop you up bit by bit till you die from the injuries.'

'That is the threat they have already made, but I will never give them what they want. They can kill me as slowly as they like, but in the end, I will be the winner. I will get my reward in the kingdom of heaven.'

Alcuin pressed his hand to the bishop's forehead and muttered, 'It's as I feared. You have a fever.'

'What do I care about that?' Sigburt said, batting Alcuin's hand away.

'All the same, I'll get you some water. You must do what you can to keep your strength up.'

Alcuin reached for the small pottery bowl of water they were given once a day. It was nearly empty, but he held what remained to the bishop's lips and was relieved when the old man drank it.

'If I die, go to Rome and tell them... tell them I was martyred.'

'I will, Your Grace.'

There was no point in saying they were unlikely to get out of this place, but there was also no point in arguing with the bishop.

'Swear it! Swear in God's name that you'll do it.'

'I swear in the name of God. I will go to Rome and tell them what happened to you.'

Alcuin and Galen had been forced on this trip by the bishop who wanted to show Galen off to the pope. If they'd been allowed to do what they wanted, Alcuin and Galen would have headed straight home to the Abbey of Yarmwick after they'd completed their commission for the king. Even now, when Alcuin had been considering escape, it had been with the intention of heading home.

Now the bishop had sworn him to a new path. One he wasn't thrilled to be on. But there was no point in saying any of that.

So Alcuin merely helped the old man to lie down again, which was difficult as he kept a tight grip on his left hand with his right.

'Good. Good man,' Sigburt said. 'And take Galen with you.'

'I don't think a trip to Rome would be a good idea. It would be best to take him straight home.'

Alcuin immediately regretted saying that. What was the point of worrying the bishop with a hypothetical situation?

'No!' Sigburt pushed himself upright, tugging on Alcuin. 'He must go to Rome. He will go to Rome!'

'He may not even be alive anymore,' Alcuin said, although the words cost him a great deal.

'Then you must take his body. He's a saint. He can't be left here to be desecrated by heathens.'

'Do you really believe that he is a saint?'

'I have seen him perform a miracle, something that I never thought I'd see in my lifetime. I know he is a saint.

But if you value your life and his, you will never tell the Moors that.'

'Of course not.'

At least Alcuin could reassure the bishop about that. He had no intention of saying Galen was a saint to anyone, least of all the Moors.

'Good,' Sigburt murmured and allowed Alcuin to lower him into a sleeping position on the ledge.

Alcuin wondered what he could do about the bishop's wound. He didn't have any medicines or light to examine it. There wasn't really anything to do, imprisoned as they both were. The bishop, thankfully, expected nothing from him and just squeezed his eyes shut, muttering prayers under his breath.

The shriek of the upper gate so soon after the bishop's return made Alcuin stiffen. It wasn't time for their food and after days in the dark he'd worked out that he and the bishop were the only ones down there. Did this mean it was his turn to be tortured?

For one mad instant he looked about the cell for a place to hide. There was nowhere. Besides, they knew he was in the cell, so they'd haul him out even if there was a hiding place.

Then he thought he might fling the contents of the pot they used as a toilet at anyone coming for him. No, that was stupid. Such behaviour was likely to make his treatment more severe. It was best not to antagonise his captors. By this point the light coming down the stairs had grown brighter than was normal when the soldiers came and went with the bishop.

Then, much to Alcuin's surprise, the urbane Moorish leech who had treated Galen stepped into the cavernous space. Two guards accompanied him with the usual torches but also two slaves carrying a pair of lanterns. Hatim stopped before Alcuin's cell and looked him up and down.

Alcuin stood in the glare of more light than he'd seen in days and felt shabby, unkempt and unprepared for whatever was to come next. Hatim relayed a command in a perfectly ordinary tone of voice and the guards hurried to open the cell door.

He stepped inside, followed by the slaves. One man held his lantern above the bishop's bed. The other placed his on the floor and held out the bag he had slung across his body.

'I've come to treat your bishop,' Hatim said.

His face twitched with distaste but Alcuin couldn't work out whether that was because of the smell, the darkness or a dislike of treating a foreigner.

'I see,' Alcuin said, although he wasn't sure he did.

Either way, he stepped back till he was pressed against the furthest wall. He was still so close the guards at the entrance could have reached out to grab him.

'I need nothing from you!' Sigburt snapped and curled his shoulders as if his back could hold the Moor at bay.

'If I don't treat your wound, it is more likely to putrefy.'

'So be it. I will accept whatever God sees fit for me.'

'What if your God sent me to heal you?'

Alcuin gasped at the absurdity of the suggestion.

But the bishop asked, 'Are you a Christian?'

'I am not,' Hatim said. 'However, I am a doctor and your chances for recovery would be better with my help.'

'Until tomorrow when your uncle will chop off another of my fingers, huh?'

'He wouldn't do that if you just handed over the treasure.'

'Never. I will never do that.'

Hatim shrugged and said something to the slaves and they started packing up what they'd already taken out.

'If that is your wish, I will leave,' Hatim said and turned to go.

'Wait!' Alcuin took a step forward and was blocked by a guard. 'Can you give me any news of Brother Galen?'

'Do you want news?' Hatim said, tilting his head as if he was considering the question.

'Is he still alive?' Alcuin asked, dreading the answer.

His face may have given him away, for the Moor's expression softened.

'He is still alive.'

'Thank God.'

It was astonishing how much relief that news gave Alcuin. It was as if he'd been holding himself rigid in anticipation and now he went soft and shaky as the fear was released. The Moor examined him with deepening curiosity.

'Come, I want a word with you.'

'Me?' Alcuin said, back to fearing he was about to be tortured.

'Who else? But not here. I can't stand the air in this fetid place.'

So Alcuin followed the Moor and was followed by the slaves and the guards as the entire group went up the long flight of stairs and out into the training ground beyond.

It surprised him to find that it was a bright, warm day up here. The sky was a deep and cloudless blue and, more astonishing still, high, snow-covered mountains loomed over the palace to the east. How had he not noticed them when he'd first arrived? Then again, he'd had too many worries at the time to look around.

Thoughts of escape were brief and quickly extinguished. The stone wall of this palace was higher, thicker and better guarded than anything he'd seen before. The palace grounds were also full of armed men engaged in strenuous training.

A particularly striking group on horseback was the first to catch his eye. A man armed with a bow was galloping at full speed across the courtyard. As he got to the midpoint of the yard he rose in his stirrups and shot an arrow into a circular target, one of a row of them, made from thick straw. The arrow plunged into the target with a thud just short of the bullseye. The man wheeled his horse about and started trotting back to the group and another horseman headed off on the same run. As his horse gathered speed he shot not one arrow but a series of three, one after the other, into the row of targets. Every one of them plunged deep into the densely packed straw.

'Mother of God,' Alcuin said.

'Mamluks,' Hatim said, following Alcuin's astonished gaze. 'The cream of the army. I'll wager you've never seen warriors like them.'

Alcuin hadn't and was angry at himself for showing how impressed he was.

'We have mighty warriors, too. My whole family are–'

Best not to mention that he was the son of an ealdorman. That needed to be held back until they were out of other options. But Alcuin had the worrying feeling that his rank would mean nothing to the Moor either way.

'They're all slaves, mainly Turks, but with some men taken from the frozen north,' Hatim said, tilting his head towards the Mamluks.

'You have slaves fighting for you? How can you ensure their loyalty if they aren't part of your family or clan?'

Hatim gave him an amused smile, as if he was dealing with someone incredibly naïve.

'Our greatest rivals for power come from within our own families. It is far safer to have an army made up of men entirely loyal to the leader. We train Mamluks from a very young age into their role. Because we separate them from their family as children they are loyal only to their trainer and their master.

'But enough about them.' Hatim turned to examine Alcuin, and the other men formed a loose circle about them. 'You and the young monk... you said you were friends.'

'Friends and brothers in Christ.'

Alcuin wondered why the Moor was starting with this and not with the bishop's treasure.

'Have you known him long?'

'A few years now.'

'So you know him well?'

'Yes, look, what's this all about? What's wrong with Galen?'

The man was making Alcuin increasingly concerned.

'I was hoping you could tell me what's wrong,' Hatim said, with that same thoughtful gaze fixed on Alcuin's face. 'He trembles and shakes when I'm in the room. He closes his eyes and nearly bursts into tears when my cousins supervise his bath, even though they are young and pretty.

Yet he does not try to stop us. He doesn't fight us or make a complaint. No harsh words pass his lips he–'

Hatim stopped, probably because Alcuin was staring wide-eyed at him.

'What? What have I done?'

'Your cousins... they're female, are they?' Alcuin asked in a voice made soft with amazement.

'Yes, A'isha and Jariya.'

'And er... when they supervise his bath, Galen is naked, is he?'

'Of course. How else could they get him clean? And how else could I examine him and make sure he is healing properly?'

'O Lordy,' Alcuin murmured. 'Poor Galen.'

'Poor Galen? What have I done that makes you say that?'

Alcuin had his doubts about telling their captors anything. Then again, if he could help Galen he had to speak out. At least only Hatim, and none of the surrounding men, would understand what he was saying.

'Well, first, you are probably not aware that our order forbids us to touch, or be touched by, any woman, even family.'

'But they are not touching him. They wouldn't want to either.'

'All the same, they are present.'

'I see.'

'Second,' Alcuin said, relieved that at least the Moor was listening, 'Galen has been ill for a very long time. So ill that it has sapped him of his strength. He can't fight you off. If he tried, he would injure himself and start to bleed so he doesn't fight.

'Third, Galen is deeply uncomfortable around strangers, afraid even. Because he's shy he sinks in on himself and locks things up inside. He wouldn't tell you, even if you were threatening him with torture, that he's struggling just to be in the presence of strangers.

'And finally, you know he was raped. It makes him wary of any touch, no matter who it comes from. He flinches every time somebody touches him, even his own father. So... do you understand why what you are doing to him, all you strangers working on his naked body, would be a severe ordeal for him?'

'I see.' Hatim threw his head back and stared at the sky while he stroked his beard. 'But if he is so shy and self-effacing, what is he doing going on a journey to Rome?'

Alcuin tried to look relaxed whilst his mind raced for a sufficient answer that omitted miracles.

'He wasn't given a choice. He's the best scribe in our land, as I am the best illuminator. Our bishop wanted us to accompany him to Rome so that we could produce a codex for the pope to celebrate the coming millennium and also to give us an opportunity to study in some of the great libraries of Rome. Galen is also a fine scholar.'

The change he saw in Hatim at mention of their professions surprised Alcuin. It seemed as though the two of them rose in the Moor's estimation, which up till this point had barely scraped interest. Although his next words were hardly encouraging.

'It seems odd to me.'

Hatim's voice reflected his disbelief and he went back to staring at Alcuin who shifted uneasily, but kept his face as neutral as he could. He knew better than to jump in and fill the space the Moor had left for him. Alcuin had to choose his words carefully and make sure he said nothing contradictory.

'It took a lot to convince Galen to take the trip. It was only because I am also on this journey that he agreed to it.'

'He must trust you a great deal.'

'He does.' It surprised Alcuin that he knew it for the truth. 'Just as I trust him. Please, don't think him a coward. He has his own bravery when it comes to protecting his friends.'

'What do you mean?'

Sweat trickled down Alcuin's temple and he wasn't sure whether it was from the unbearable heat of the sun or the pressure of this interrogation. Hatim spoke mildly, but his questions were to the point and he wasn't missing a word or inflection.

So Alcuin tried to pick his way carefully through the story of their first encounter with the vikings. It felt so long ago and maybe telling this Moor that Galen was brave was a mistake, but he wanted to give Galen some dignity at least.

'He knew he couldn't make it, you see? He knew he was holding me up, so he threatened to kill himself to force me to leave him behind. That took more courage than many a warrior might show.'

'Mmm,' Hatim said, 'to commit such an act for a friend, that is a fine thing, certainly.'

'He has his own bravery. Just not when dealing with strangers. Familiar faces always surrounded him till he left home. Then he moved to the monastery where he was certain he'd remain for the rest of his life. So being forced on this journey, well... it's been difficult for him.'

'I am impressed by your defence of him.'

Alcuin nodded, uncertain whether his tale had done Galen any good. He also wished he could ask more about Galen and beg to see him.

'You should be careful,' Hatim said. 'Your concern for your friend appears to be more important than your concern for yourself. It might make people wonder why.'

'If you got to know him well you might feel the same,' Alcuin said, for he'd seen more than one person won over by Galen's non-judgemental acceptance.

'Perhaps, but you have also shown me a way to control you, and I wonder whether a threat to you would be as effective in controlling Brother Galen.'

Alcuin gasped as he stared at the Moor. He'd been a fool to be so open. He'd been trying to win some understanding for Galen and instead he'd put both of them in even more danger.

'Why do you need to control us more? We are already entirely at your mercy.'

'Because it might loosen your tongue when it comes to the second treasure.'

'I swear, upon my life and upon my God, I know nothing about the second treasure and neither does Galen.'

'Then you'd better find a way to make yourselves useful before my uncle decides you are not worth the expense of feeding.'

'Something like what?' Alcuin was surprised that the Moor had even given him this hint. It made him suspect the man wanted him and Galen, or at least Galen, for his own purposes.

'I leave that up to you.'

'I have already asked the bishop about the second treasure. He refuses to tell me what it is.'

'You would betray him in that way?'

'I don't see the point of withholding some worldly good at the cost of his life and ours.'

'But maybe it isn't a worldly good,' Hatim said with a sardonic smile.

'What else could it be?'

'That's for you to discover. Failing that, a conversion to the one true faith may be the only thing to save you,' Hatim said and walked off.

Alcuin stared back at him in shock and barely registered as a guard took a tight grip of his arm and pushed him back into the dungeons. So he had two choices now: betray the bishop or convert. No, probably only one: betray the bishop and convert. That or escape.

Chapter 6

A loud piercing cry that left him wide-eyed, gasping for breath and with his heart hammering against his ribs, shocked Galen out of sleep. It was light in the room and for a moment he thought he must have dreamed the sound, but then he heard it again.

It was a mixture of a cat mewing and a baby's cry. He'd been hearing the same thing for a while, but had yet to work out what it was. It was closer today and he was certain he didn't want to come across any creature that made such a sinister noise.

To distract and calm himself, Galen took to tracing the pattern on the floor with his eyes. The central bit had a rectangular section inlaid with coloured tiles that gave the appearance of a jewelled tapestry. The pattern was similar to the star overhead, but had yellows as well as greens and blues. They repeated endlessly and with such complexity that Galen could make smaller and greater repeating patterns starting with the single elements of triangles, then joining them together with the white lines to make larger diamonds that in turn could be joined into a larger same-coloured stripes that ran the full length of the rectangle.

Galen wondered, for the hundredth time, where Alcuin was and whether he too had such a marvel to keep his mind occupied. An artist like him would find these designs fascinating. Wondering about Alcuin brought back Galen's dread and despair over his current situation but Alcuin would tell him to focus on getting better instead. That was what he had to do for both their sakes.

The sound of footsteps drew Galen's attention to the door. He tensed, expecting the usual crowd of women, slaves and Hatim. But today, Hatim was the only one to step into the room.

Galen's anxiety rose, as it did whenever there was a change, and he watched Hatim approach the bed. He never knew what the Moor was thinking. He couldn't stop himself from pulling his covers up to his chin either, even though it would provide no defence.

'Good morning,' Hatim said as he pulled up a cushion and settled too close for Galen's comfort.

It was a strange habit of the Moors that they sat about cross-legged on the floor. Once Hatim was comfortable he placed the back of his hand against Galen's forehead to check his temperature, then held out his hand. Galen had become so used to this that he slipped his hand out from under the blanket so that Hatim could take his pulse.

'Good, much improved,' Hatim said. 'You have more colour in your cheeks too. How is the pain?'

'It is less,' Galen said, surprised and relieved, for he'd found it difficult to believe that anything Hatim had done would help. 'I was able to roll onto my side this morning too,' he added, flushing with embarrassment that he was proud of such a paltry achievement.

'I continue to be impressed by your recovery,' Hatim said. 'Now, I have brought you something.'

'My clothes?' Galen said hopefully.

'Your books.'

Hatim pulled the two codices out of a voluminous pocket and laid them on Galen's bed.

Galen couldn't stop the sigh of relief at seeing his books. Yet he didn't dare take them. He wasn't sure why the Moor had brought them, nor what game he might play with them. Although, to give the man his due, he'd been reasonably straightforward with Galen until now.

His fingers itched to touch the reassuringly familiar leather covers, but for now he'd wait. Hatim gave him a cynical smile as if he understood what Galen was thinking. He did that rather often.

'I had a chat with your friend, Brother Alcuin, to find out why you were so uncomfortable in my presence and with my examinations.'

'You did?' Galen was relieved to hear that Alcuin was still around and able to have something as mundane as a chat. 'Is he well?'

'Your friend is fine. He also explained that your vows prevent you from being touched by women.'

'Oh,' Galen said, and flushed bright red.

'They don't touch you, but they observe and I can see how that might make you uncomfortable. You could have told me.'

'Could I?' Galen asked, and the familiar sick tide of panic rose in his chest as it always did when Hatim cross-examined him.

'We too have holy men who don't touch women.'

'So you... you won't have your cousins around when you are washing me anymore?'

'I won't. You see, I am a doctor. My interest is in your wellbeing; in healing you. I have no wish to harm or distress you.'

'And what of later?'

'Later?'

Hatim's expression of slight interest didn't so much as flicker and his voice remained calm and even, like an adult talking to an anxious child. It did nothing to allay Galen's fear.

'Once I am healed as far as you can manage. What will happen then?'

'That will be up to my uncle to decide.'

'Your uncle?'

'And your bishop,' Hatim said, stroking his beard with a hand that had a ring on every finger, and sometimes two. 'He is refusing to give up the second treasure. Even when my uncle has threatened to chop his fingers and hands off, he remains stubborn.'

Galen gave a start of fright that he hoped wasn't noticed and he pulled the covers more tightly around his neck. He wondered how a man who called himself a doctor could speak so calmly of torture.

'Maybe it doesn't exist.'

The words escaped Galen's lips before he could think better of it. It was always the same, and even though he mistrusted the bishop, he couldn't let them torture him without reason.

'Do you think so?' Hatim asked as he reached for an engraved brass mug, topped it up with water from a similarly patterned brass pitcher and made a gesture with his hand, indicating Galen should sit up.

It surprised Galen that Hatim was providing this service. Usually he left such menial activities to his slaves or his cousins. He wouldn't keep Hatim waiting, so Galen used his pillows to ease himself up sufficiently to take a sip. Then he realised Hatim was also waiting for an answer to his question.

'I know nothing about the second treasure. Alcuin and I were never in Bishop Sigburt's confidence.'

'You don't care for him?'

'I hardly know him.'

'You don't?'

Galen shook his head.

'He wanted me and Alcuin for his own purposes. Beyond that, we held no interest for him. We are just youngest sons and he is a powerful man with a strong sense of destiny.'

'Youngest sons? What has that to say about anything?'

The question threw Galen because to him it was self-evident why he and Alcuin were less important.

'Um... we don't inherit and I have a handful of brothers ahead of me so I am unlikely to ever inherit. I am just a burden to my family.'

'Ah,' Hatim said. 'I forgot about that Christian system of yours. Amongst my people, the order of birth is irrelevant.'

'It is? So how do you choose a successor to your leader?'

'The leader names his successor, whomever he deems to be the best person for the job. If it were any other way, I'd have no chance to succeed my uncle.'

'You wouldn't?'

Galen was confused and uncertain as to the relevance of the conversation. He got the impression Hatim just liked to talk. But he had to be careful not to let down his guard no matter how innocuous the conversation felt, lest he let slip something Hatim could use against him.

'I wouldn't be in line,' Hatim said. 'Tell me, how many brothers do you have?'

'Four,' Galen said. 'And I have three sisters.'

Hatim waved his hand as if sisters counted for nothing.

'These siblings, you all have the same mother, not so?'

'Well, yes, we are fortunate that our mother is still with us, so my father has not remarried.'

'I have one hundred and thirty-two half-brothers. My father, too, had a similar number of brothers. My uncle inherited the governorship of this town from my father, and I am fortunate that my uncle has seen fit to name me as his successor, even though I am not my father's eldest son. Nevertheless, the succession won't come about without some intrigue, so I keep a watchful eye on all my potential rivals.'

'A hundred and thirty-two brothers?'

Galen could barely comprehend such a figure. His entire extended family of uncles and cousins didn't come to such a number.

Hatim gave an amused snort and said, 'Since you are the youngest and, according to your own estimation, not important, why were you with the bishop? Are you his staff?'

Galen gave Hatim a dubious stare. He felt like the Moor already knew the answer.

'I'm a scribe. One day I hope also to be a translator, and Alcuin, well... he is a great artist. If you give him some paints and parchment, he will produce the most beautiful things for you.'

Hatim nodded, not looking surprised, which confirmed Galen's suspicion that he was merely double-checking something he already knew.

'So this work you two do, it's not as simple as the two books you own?'

'Not at all,' Galen hurried to assure him. 'Alcuin... his art is like nothing I've ever seen before.'

'You interest me. Why are you telling me so much about your friend?'

'Because I don't want you to hurt him. If... if you cut off his hands you would deprive the world of so many beautiful things it... it would be terrible.'

'We have no intention of cutting off his hands. Honestly, why do you behave as though we are some barbaric tribe? I mean, look around you. Does anything in your miserable land come close to what you see here?'

'It is very fine. I have... I have seen nothing to equal it but you... you have threatened to cut off our bishop's hand already.'

'And you are telling me that your people don't do the same?'

'No, I'm not saying that.'

Galen swallowed hard, because Hatim looked angry. Then, as if he'd noticed Galen's increased dread, he sighed and his shoulders and face relaxed again.

'You should try to stand up for yourself.'

'What?'

'Try being firmer with people. You could have saved yourself a great deal of embarrassment if you'd told me not to let women touch you.'

'I asked, but you didn't listen,' Galen said, his voice filled with apprehension.

Hatim's brows snapped together, and he looked to be thinking.

'You had to be cleaned so that I could check on the progress of your healing.'

Galen gave a slight nod.

'People don't listen to me.'

'How can you speak in such a matter-of-fact way? I can't imagine anything more irritating than to be ignored.'

'Look at me,' Galen said with a faint, embarrassed smile. 'If you came upon me unexpectedly and I stood between you and your prize, would anything I had to say stop you?'

'I don't suppose it would. Your reasoning is sound, but doesn't it enrage you to be so disregarded?'

'What can I do about it?'

'Stand up for yourself!' Hatim said and was so exercised by the idea he sprang to his feet and strode about the room.

'It isn't in my nature. Other small, scrawny men fight their way to the top, suffer blows both physical and verbal and use the force of their personalities to cow far more powerful men, but I can't do that. I feel sick just to be in a room where others are arguing. I have no bravery.'

'That isn't what your friend tells me.'

'Alcuin is a kind and loyal friend but he knows the number of times he's had to support me just so I could appear in a room full of people I don't know.'

Galen shuddered as he remembered all the times he'd been sick with dread in his father's and the king's hall.

Hatim just looked astonished.

'I have a cousin, a shy little girl, timid as a mouse. She quivers and shakes and hides behind her mother's skirts, but I have never come across a man who is the same.'

Galen flushed, and his gaze dropped to the floor. This wasn't the first time someone had compared him to a maiden, but it was still embarrassing.

'I have touched a nerve,' Hatim said, coming back to settle on his cushion. 'So I will change the subject. Tell me more about your two books and why you took them, rather than any other.'

'Oh,' Galen said, and finally gathered the courage to touch his two books. They'd had a rough journey and the leather felt dry and cracked against his fingertips. 'The first is just my notebook. I've had it since I was a boy. I used it for practising my lessons at first and later for writing down my thoughts and trying my hand at translation.'

'That would explain the random nature of what I found. Much of it in your own language, I gather.'

'Yes.'

'And the other book? The one by Boethius on rhetoric?'

'It was an exchange. Given to me by a man I taught to write. It was a family heirloom.'

'So you, a monk who should own nothing, took someone's most precious possession?'

'No, no, it's nothing like that. I translated this book into Englisc, and he asked to keep the version he could actually understand. Then he gave me the original.'

'I apologise for my mistake.' Hatim eased the book out of Galen's hand and flipped it open. 'It's an interesting read, and not a book I had come across before.'

'It's useful for rulers,' Galen said, gazing wistfully at the book and praying it would be returned to him once Hatim was done. It surprised him that the Moor had read the book in the brief time he'd had it.

'It's also useful for priests, or anyone who wishes to hold the attention of a crowd. Is that the kind of thing you want to translate?'

'What?' Galen said, looking up in confusion.

'You said you wanted to become a translator. What would you translate?'

'I'd like to translate the works of the ancients from their original Latin into Englisc.'

'What sorts of works?'

'Any of them,' Galen said with a slight shrug.

'You wouldn't stick to religious works?'

'No, why?'

'Because Christians seem not to hold with some of the ancient knowledge. You call it heresy.'

'I doubt a monastery would hold heretical books.'

Galen wasn't so confident about what he was saying. He sometimes wondered about the books that he came across in the abbey's library. But he'd decided that if they were within the walls of his holy institution he would be safe enough to read and even transcribe them.

Hatim though, was too perceptive and gave a loud 'Ha!' Then, keeping his eagle-like gaze upon Galen, he said, 'You are trying to keep your voice and face expressionless. Is this a sign of rebellion from you, little monk? Am I to understand that you are determined to read anything you come upon, no matter what your church rules?'

'What?'

The accusation, and the sense that Hatim might be right, shocked Galen. Another sign, if he needed one, to show he wasn't a saint. No saint would be rebellious and doubtful about his own church's teachings.

'I have hit a nerve.' Hatim looked smug as he handed the book back to Galen. 'But I won't push you on this matter today. Instead, let us consider the future. Would you translate anything out of Arabic? My uncle's palace has a vast library.'

This came as such a surprise that Galen could do little more than blink at Hatim for a while.

'I can't speak Arabic.'

'Would you like to learn?'

'Me? How?'

'I could teach you.'

'Why would you want to?'

'Because I am curious to learn this Englisc of yours.'

'You are?'

'You don't believe me?'

'Why would you want to learn a language spoken by a bunch of barbarians in some soggy backwater?'

Hatim gave a shout of surprised laughter.

'You are sharper than you let on. Let's just say for now that it might be interesting to learn a language so different from my own and from Latin.'

On the one hand, Galen wondered whether this was an as-yet-unfathomable trap. On the other, the idea of learning another language intrigued him. One, moreover, with a different alphabet. He'd have liked to consider the offer for longer, but it was clear Hatim wanted an answer now. So, despite his reservations, he gave a quick nod.

'Very well,' Hatim said, 'tomorrow I'll bring some of my books and paper and we can begin.'

Galen nodded. In this behaviour Hatim was like Alcuin. They were both men of action. No sooner did a thought occur to them than they acted upon it. This got Galen worrying about Alcuin yet again and he was squeezing up his courage to ask whether he could see his friend when an astonishing creature strutted in through the courtyard entrance.

It was a bird, perhaps as big as a swan, but taller. The thick feathers of its neck glistened in iridescent green and a blue so intense it was almost the definition of blue itself. It turned its head in the strange jerking motion of all birds which set the crown of dot-like feathers floating above its head to waggling. Then it raised its long tail and fanned it open. An army of hundreds of eyes transfixed Galen. These started to shake with a loud and ominous hissing sound.

'God preserve me,' Galen whispered and made the sign of the cross to ward off the terrifying creature.

'Get out, you bastard!' Hatim shouted, as he swept the water jug off the table and flung it at the bird.

It landed with a deafening crash at the animal's feet, bounced, twirled and clattered, splashing water everywhere.

The bird gave an ear-shattering shriek and stalked back into the courtyard, its tail feathers shaking aggressively.

'What was that?'

Galen was trembling with shock as he pulled the covers back up to his chin.

'It's one of my uncle's damned peacocks. They're a bloody nuisance, but he likes them both as an ornament for his gardens and as food for his table. I can't stand them, especially their cry. They jolt me out of my contemplation at the most inopportune moments.'

The door swung open before Galen could say anything and Jariya walked in, followed by the angelic-looking guard with the sword and the dagger. Now that she and her sister would no longer be supervising his baths, Galen could face her with a degree of calm, although nothing would remove his embarrassment at how both women had seen him.

Jariya raised one perfectly plucked eyebrow as she took in the water splashed across the floor and the jug still rocking back and forth on its side. She asked a question with a none-too-impressed tone of voice and got a sheepish sounding reply from Hatim before she retrieved the jug and then mopped up the spilled water.

Jariya, Galen had learned, was the eldest daughter of Hatim's uncle, Zayd Al-Ifriqi. She was the taller of the two cousins, with a longer, thinner face than her sister's. While the rest of her clothes changed, silk dresses of a range of different colours and patterns, her pearl fringed veil always remained the same. She had a serious demeanour and never seemed to smile.

Her younger sister had more of a heart-shaped face, boundless energy and a playful nature. Although Galen couldn't understand what the women said, she always seemed to be joking around with Hatim.

Galen was usually drawn to cheerful, friendly people but he felt a sense of sympathy and fellow feeling for Jariya. It was meaningless, of course. He was a prisoner in this palace and her family's captive. If anyone was deserving of sympathy, it was Galen. He knew he wouldn't get it, but maybe learning Arabic would be helpful beyond the merely academic exercise he'd first considered it to be.

CHAPTER 7

Alcuin tried to establish a routine to fill his days and distract his mind. The terror of what was to come would overwhelm him if all he did was sit in the dark and think. Dread for himself and concern for Galen, all alone in this strange land, consumed him.

Now he took the arrival of food as the start of his day. He followed his meagre meal with prayer, reciting the nine offices of the day, beginning with prime. By his reckoning he'd been down here for three weeks. He interspersed that with pacing the cell to maintain his fitness and in between he saw to the bishop's needs. The old man had lost three fingers now, and he'd developed a fever.

'Perhaps you should allow their leech to look after your wounds, Your Grace,' Alcuin said as he mopped the sweat from the bishop's brow.

'Never. I will never let that godless man lay a hand on me.'

'It might buy you some time.'

'I put my faith in God. I need nothing else.'

Alcuin suppressed a sigh. They seemed always to be arguing over the same thing. He folded away the rag he'd been using on the bishop and went back to pacing. The cell was exactly six steps long and four and a half wide. He stuck to the length when the bishop was there. He did the width, including stepping up onto the bishop's bed-like ledge and back down again when the old man wasn't there.

'Must you keep pacing?'

Sigburt's voice was heavy with irritation, made sharper because they both knew the guards would shortly appear to take the bishop away for another round of interrogation. The sound of the outer door crashing open punctuated the sentence and the two prisoners fell silent, listening to the guards coming down the stairs. Neither man moved as their cell door was swung open.

Sigburt was determined to be uncooperative to the last. The guards were so familiar with this that they no longer bothered to shout their orders, incomprehensible as they were. The bigger man simply grabbed the bishop by his robe, hauled him to his feet and thrust him out into the hall.

Then, much to Alcuin's surprise, the other guard grabbed Alcuin's arm and hauled him out of the cell, too.

'Dear God in heaven, help your servant in his hour of need,' Alcuin muttered, certain that his time to be tortured had come.

He tried to get the shakes that threatened to overwhelm him under control as he followed the bishop. Sigburt was so worn down and resigned to his fate that he no longer shook or moaned or shed the tears that Alcuin still did. At the very least, Alcuin thought, he should follow the old man's lead and hang on to as much dignity as he could.

That nearly made him laugh. He'd seen men being tortured. There was never any dignity involved.

Still, he needed to prepare his mind as best he could and he took deep measured breaths as they walked him and the bishop into the massive palace. The size of the place still overwhelmed him. In his present state of mind, it oppressed him and made him feel it would be impossible to withstand anything the people who could produce such awe-inspiring buildings could throw at him.

He barely glanced at the wonders of the highly polished and reflective marble floors, the walls that were so richly decorated they looked like glowing manuscripts, nor the carved and painted archways and courtyards they passed through. All he could do was keep his eyes fixed on the back of the bishop's head as he prayed for strength.

Then they stopped at a particularly grand entrance. There was the unfamiliar Arabic script carved into the lintel above the doors. Piles of shoes littered the floor at the entrance, which made no sense.

Then the sound of music distracted him and he looked beyond the shoes into something approaching a long hall, although it was far wider, taller, and flooded with light. They'd covered the floor with thick colourful carpets woven in a mixture of geometric and curvaceous patterns. Men sat cross-legged on those carpets to either side of the door.

Dotted amongst them were others seated on cushions that elevated them above the masses. Right at the far end, opposite the door, on a carved throne above all the other men, sat the dark-skinned old Moor. To his left, a group of women sat on the floor playing a variety of unfamiliar instruments, the source of the music. The hum of conversation dropped away as the bishop was pushed into the room.

Alcuin expected to follow him but the guard that remained prodded him further along the corridor, up a wide sweep of stairs, along another corridor, up a narrower flight of stairs to a narrower corridor and past a series of normal, human-sized doors, till he was brought to a halt at the entrance to a plain room. The room had a threadbare carpet and a stack of blankets folded in one corner. A low table and a cushion were set beside the shuttered window.

The guard shoved him into the room so hard he went flying across it and only stopped as he crashed into the desk, cracking his shins and flailing about so as not to fall over. The door behind him slammed shut and a lock clicked. Alcuin spun round, his eyes watering from the pain in his shins, and stared at the door. He was alone.

For form's sake, for he was certain there was no escape possible, Alcuin tested the door. It wasn't as solid as he'd expected. The lock wobbled and felt like it might be possible to break it, given a bit of work.

Then he went to the window. Lattice-work wooden shutters closed it off, but bright shafts of light pierced the geometric pattern of squares and circles. The shutters were simply on a latch, and Alcuin cautiously pulled them open. Solid vertical bars prevented any escape, but this was a far better prison than the one he'd been holed up in until now.

Alcuin looked down first and hastily backed away. He was so high up! How could any building be so high? And so vast. He was in a sort of cloister and assumed that what he saw on the opposite side reflected the room he was in. So he was on the top floor, and what looked like cells, but of a monastery rather than a prison, formed this entire floor. Below him was a short section of terracotta roof tiles, and below that were two more floors of covered and many-columned walkways. In the centre was a courtyard.

Alcuin could only see the furthest edge, but it appeared to be filled with an unfamiliar, leathery, dark green tree.

He pulled at the bars, but they didn't budge. Although rain had caused a stain of rust on the plaster into which the bottom of the bars were fixed, the bars themselves were thick and not corroded. A swift shrieked past his window so unexpectedly that Alcuin jumped and jerked back, cursing as he did so.

His nerves were stretched thin. How could a bird give him a fright? Now that he looked he could see hundreds of them, swooping about above the cloister, pausing only briefly at a nest made of clay that clung to the underside of the roof, to feed their squealing chicks. Beyond the cloud of swifts were the mountains, the taller ones still covered in snow and above that, the sky, that in this land seemed always to be free of clouds and a clear deep blue.

How Alcuin wished he could be a bird, slip through the bars and fly away. Alas, that was not to be. He wondered why they'd taken him to this better room. It might be a prison, but it was one with light, clean air and a degree more comfort.

Did the two blankets indicate he was to have company? Would it be the bishop or Galen? He hoped it would be Galen, but he doubted it. And the desk... What was the desk about?

The loud clunk of the lock made Alcuin jump again. So much could happen next, and his frantic brain could barely fathom what it could be or what he should do about it.

The Moor, Hatim, stepped into the room and looked Alcuin up and down, while the slave who followed him placed a covered tray on the low table. The slave bowed and backed out of the room, leaving the door open. Alcuin briefly considered running through it but he wouldn't get far.

Even if he couldn't see a guard, they were bound to be close. Hatim was doubtless also a ruthless warrior. He certainly had the build for it.

'You are wondering why you've been moved,' Hatim said.

'Of course.'

Alcuin gave the Moor back stare for stare, fortifying himself with the thought that he was also nobility and his family's pride should be maintained.

'Your friend, Brother Galen, told me you are the finest artist in your land and, if I recall correctly, you said something similar. You must be good for your king to have summoned you.'

'And?'

'I was told by your little friend to set you a challenge.'

Hatim pulled away the cloth that covered the tray the slave had set on the table. Laid out on it with geometric precision was a row of coloured inks, brushes, quills and even a small amount of gold leaf and a stack of what Alcuin assumed was vellum, although it didn't look quite right.

'Are you setting me a commission?'

'Draw whatever you want. I doubt your skill is on a par with the artists of my uncle's land, but I may as well find out what you are capable of.'

Alcuin was astonished to be spoken to in this way. He'd never thought of himself as a vain man but to be dismissed like this was a first. He didn't like it, but bit down on his first words, which would have been something like,

I'll show you. Instead, he gave what he hoped was an unperturbed smile.

'I accept your challenge.'

The moment Hatim left he caught himself swearing under his breath and pacing the small room. Then he glanced down at all the tools he needed for this peculiar job. Maybe this was a way to avoid death.

Up till now, he and Galen and the bishop had been prisoners of little value. In a worst-case scenario, they'd be put to death because they were holy men of an opposing faith. Slightly better than that was being sold into slavery.

But if he and Galen could prove their worth, they might be taken on as servants. And, after a while, if they gained their captors' trust, their vigilance might falter. Then the two of them could attempt an escape.

For the first time in days, Alcuin felt a spark of hope. He pulled the cushion closer to the desk, positioning himself side-on to the window so that the light shone onto the thing that looked like vellum but was considerably more fibrous and slightly bumpy, and considered what he should draw.

If he didn't know how guileless Galen was, Alcuin might have thought this was his friend's plan to win freedom all along. But it was more likely the young man merely wanted Hatim to see Alcuin's art. Either way, Alcuin said a prayer of thanks to Galen and to God to have been given this chink of hope.

Chapter 8

The sound of rain in the courtyard and gusts of wind intruded into Galen's dreams. He opened his eyes to work out what was making the noise and was amazed by the ferocity of the downpour. It was as if a giant was tipping bucket after bucket of water over them. This land was so different from home. Even the rain was fiercer and heavier.

The one advantage of the storm was that the usual morning glare, which prevented Galen from seeing much through the door, was gone. Through the sheets of rain he could make out a square paved in white marble with a fountain in the centre with waves of water gushing over it. There were also plants all around the edge of the square, but they were being battered so hard by the rain that Galen still couldn't work out what they were.

Either way, it was morning and Galen took the opportunity to say his prayers while he was alone and undisturbed. As had become his habit he thanked God for keeping him alive and prayed for deliverance for Alcuin, Bishop Sigburt and himself. He worried non-stop for Alcuin and felt guilt that he cared less about the bishop.

He also apologised to God for remaining curled up on his side during his prayers. He sensed that God wouldn't mind, but felt he owed it to his Creator to give him more respect.

'I give thanks for the healing I have received too,' Galen whispered. 'Hatim says we all pray to the same God, so I hope Hatim is also under your protection.'

Galen had taken to adding the Moor into his prayers, even though it would amuse the man to hear it. Galen was still as weak as a newborn, and struggled to remain sitting upright for extended periods, but he felt less pain. It was a change for the better and one to be grateful for.

Just then the door swung open, got caught by the wind and slammed against the wall with such a loud bang it made Galen jump. Then the slaves that went everywhere with Hatim arrived. This morning they were more heavily laden with goods than usual.

Hatim followed them in and A'isha and Jariya came next, tailed by the angelic-looking guard. The women arrived with their usual implements, Jariya with her book and A'isha with her musical instrument.

'Good morning,' Hatim said, looming over Galen while the slaves laid all that Galen would need for writing on the low table beside his bed. 'Are you ready for your first lesson?'

'I am.' Galen had intended to speak louder, but nerves meant the sound of the rain nearly drowned out his words.

'Excellent, but first we need to do something about the wind and the noise,' Hatim said and spoke to his people, pointing at the pool of water that had formed on the marble outside and was threatening to flood the room.

The slaves leaped into action and pulled a door shut that Galen hadn't even realised existed. It closed off the courtyard and cut some of the wind, although not all, as the windows to either side remained open.

'Don't worry, it will soon pass. These spring rains are violent but fleeting.'

Hatim settled himself on the thick cushion opposite Galen with the table between them. A'isha sat cross-legged on the opposite bench and strummed her instrument softly. She appeared to be in a more reflective mood than usual. The music she played had a strange quality to it with oddly sliding notes that flicked suddenly to another tone. It was as unfamiliar to Galen as everything else here.

Jariya, as Galen had become used to, sat behind and slightly to one side of Hatim and held her notebook and pen at the ready. It seemed she recorded everything her cousin did. Galen had thought she was only making a record of Hatim's medical treatments, but if that were the case, why record this lesson? Honestly, Galen had more questions than answers about these people.

'Right,' Hatim said, drawing Galen's attention back to him. 'I have never taught somebody my language, and I haven't learned a new language as an adult, so I intend to use the method we employ for teaching children. I suggest, however, that we do both languages at the same time. So I'll explain a few basics of Arabic and then you can do the same for Englisc.'

'The problem is, I don't understand your alphabet,' Galen said, not wishing to raise difficulties that surely Hatim had already considered. 'While you already know the Latin alphabet.'

'So Englisc uses the Latin alphabet, does it?'

'Now, yes. Once upon a time it had a very different alphabet, but it isn't used anymore.'

'Do you know it?'

'I do.'

'Why?' Galen jumped at the directness of the question and Hatim said, 'You will get used to my abrupt ways, eventually.'

Galen's eyes widened as he considered this possibility. Would he become accustomed?

'I was curious about the script. We had a stone standing on the edge of my father's burh that had the ancient writing carved into it. So our priest taught it to me.'

'Why isn't it used anymore?'

'The church adopted Latin and all the books were in the Latin alphabet. So I suppose the monks started writing everything, even Englisc, in Latin letters.'

'Will you teach me this other alphabet?'

'If you wish it.'

'I do,' Hatim said. 'But I'll start with my language. I have brought my dictionary so that we may work on words.'

'A dictionary?'

Hatim held up a large book covered in emerald green leather with gold Arabic script embossed onto it in a large decorative square.

'It's a book that holds all the meanings of words listed in the order of how they are pronounced. So words produced from deep in the throat are first and words that come from the tip of the lips are listed last. I have not come across a dictionary for Latin but perhaps you know of such a codex for your Englisc?'

'No, I've never heard of such a thing,' Galen said, and embarrassed by how much effort it took, he pulled himself more upright on his pillows and tugged the covers up with him to hide his body.

'Are you cold?'

Galen flushed and shook his head.

'So you wrap the covers around you because you are modest?'

'I'm not used to appearing before people with no clothes,' Galen said, getting steadily redder.

'Would you like a qamisa?'

'A what?'

'This,' Hatim said, tugging at the white long-sleeved undergarment that poked out from under his overgarment at his wrist.

'Can I have my habit back?'

Galen feared he might offend Hatim if he was too forward, but needed to ask.

'Not yet. Once you have healed, I will consider it, but not yet.'

Hatim issued a command and a slave ran off.

'While he is doing that, I will introduce you to the Qur'an. It is the word of God as dictated to our prophet Mohammed by the archangel Gabriel. It is our holy book and also what we use for teaching our children how to read.'

Despite his discomfort at being in this room full of people, far from friends and family, Galen felt a spark of curiosity as he looked down at the book Hatim was holding with such reverence. The cover was a deep blue leather with a complex pattern of stylised gold Arabic letters which took pride of place in the centre. Surrounding it was a gold border in the same geometric patterns as Galen was becoming familiar with in all the decorations in his room.

'Like our Bible,' Galen said. 'We also use it to learn to read.'

'We are all peoples of the book.'

Hatim opened the Qur'an and again it was a mixture of familiarity and strangeness for Galen within the covers. It was clearly a holy book, but the script, a beautiful looping, flowing style, was entirely incomprehensible. They also decorated each page with a wide frame in red ink.

'This holy book comprises one hundred and fourteen suras, which are the sayings that guide our daily life in every aspect, from what we may eat or drink, to how we should treat other people and our holy laws.'

'It is comprehensive indeed.'

Galen was filled with curiosity to know what the book said, while he wondered whether it was permissible to read it. What was the holy church's view on the Qur'an? He had no idea, for he'd never expected to come across it.

Now here he was. He decided it was better to be informed than ignorant. Besides, he couldn't prevent Hatim from teaching him. The man's expression had grown more enthusiastic by the minute.

Either way, the return of the slave delayed the moment of revelation. He was breathless and carrying a lightweight white tunic, which he held out before him with a deep bow.

'Alright,' Hatim said. 'My slave will put it on for you.'

'I can do it myself.'

Galen was deeply relieved to finally have something to wear but cringed at the idea of anyone else dressing him.

'I doubt that. You are improving, but still very weak,' Hatim said.

Galen pushed himself more upright, to prove that he could not only sit unaided but also dress himself. But the slave obeyed Hatim's abrupt order and slipped the tunic over Galen's head while Galen held up the covers to preserve his modesty.

It should have made no difference since Hatim had frequently seen him naked. But he still found it uncomfortable, especially as the two women paused, one at her writing and the other playing her musical instrument, to watch him dress. Then the slave added a few more cushions so that Galen could sit upright. The position caused a dull ache in his belly, but it was one he was able to ignore.

'Those circular scars with the cut in the middle that cover your body?' Hatim said. 'Were they caused by your king's physician?'

'How do you know about him?' Galen wrapped his arms around his body as the question brought back terrible memories. 'The king's leech would make a cut, warm a glass cup over a flame and place it over the wound and it would suck blood out of my body.'

'I am aware of the technique of cupping, although the glass shouldn't be heated to the point where it burns the skin and leaves a mark. Why was he doing it to you?'

'When I bleed, it often brings on a fever. He said drawing blood would prevent the fever,' Galen said with a shudder.

'So... you were losing blood and this leech was removing even more?'

Galen gave a quick nod.

'How did it make you feel?' Hatim asked and was back to examining Galen like he was a mere medical curiosity.

'I wasn't able... to reason clearly at the time, but I thought... I thought he might kill me.'

'So you stopped him?'

'Alcuin did. Irminric wouldn't listen to me.'

'I see.'

Galen grimaced, and he looked down and became distracted by the tunic.

'It's a very fine cloth.'

'It's cotton. My slave obviously doesn't think you deserve better. I assure you I would never wear something so inferior.'

Galen's eyes flitted over Hatim's clothes. Today's tunic was a thicker silk fabric in an iron blue that had a gleam even in the grey light of the rainy day. The broad borders of his collar, cuffs and around the upper arm were embroidered in a pattern of Arabic text in a silver thread that oozed opulence.

'This undershirt is much better than anything I've ever worn.'

'Except that you have a very fine cloak.'

'You have my cloak?'

Galen looked up anxiously and then hastily looked away again, trying to appear unconcerned so that Hatim wouldn't wonder about the cloak or decide to keep it.

'Now, why does your cloak interest you more than the knowledge that I have the rest of your clothes?'

'My father gave me that cloak. It has no more importance than that.'

Hatim's eyebrows arched in surprise, and Galen knew he looked more discomforted confessing this than anything else. He was also giving Hatim more knowledge about himself than was wise.

'You are to be congratulated that your father gives you such fine gifts. As you know, my father has already died, although my uncle treats me with great affection.'

'And your mother?' Galen asked and wondered whether women were as dismissed in this society as in his own. Perhaps not as much, since his cousins constantly followed Hatim around.

'Happily, my mother is still alive and lives here in my uncle's harem. She is a Christian woman, a younger daughter of the old King of Leon.'

'Your mother's a Christian?' Galen said, considerably surprised, although he supposed that explained Hatim's blue eyes.

'My father was an Arab, though, which gives me greater status. My uncle's mother was a Berber woman, hence his darker skin.'

'But... how did a Christian woman land up being married to a follower of Islam and be living in a harem? Isn't that a place where your leader keeps his wives? Did your uncle marry your mother?' Galen blurted out, so filled with curiosity that he couldn't stop himself.

Hatim burst out laughing and said, 'You people of Christendom have a strange notion of what a harem is. It is merely the part of the home where all the women and children live. As for my mother, she is not married to my uncle, but she is a part of his household. She married my father to seal an alliance. It is one advantage of being able to have more than one wife—that you can form more alliances through marriage.'

'I see.'

Galen stared at Hatim in more surprise than he had up till now. This truly was a mysterious new world and provided a great deal of food for thought.

'It is also why I am currently accompanied by my cousins,' Hatim said, sweeping his arm about the room to encompass Jariya and A'isha. 'It will secure my place as my uncle's heir if I marry one of his daughters.'

'You'd marry a cousin?'

'We have no strictures against it.'

'Do you want to marry one of them?'

'I don't really mind. They are both nice enough women. I just can't decide which one to take and as they are both vying for my attention, they are being as nice as they can to me.'

'But... if you can marry more than one woman, why don't you just marry both?'

Hatim threw back his head and laughed.

'It would solve one problem, for yes, I could do that. But then there would have to be the discussion of who was the first wife and the quarrels for that would be endless, especially as the eldest would demand that as her right.'

'Your first wife?' Galen said, wondering whether Hatim's beard made him look older than he actually was.

'Did you think I already had several? Order of marriage is important. To secure my position with my uncle I had to ensure one of his daughters was my first wife. So I have waited.'

'It seems you have waited a long time.'

'Ah now, don't insult me. I am only twenty-four. And I was away studying medicine for a time, which also delayed my marriage. So now all I have to do is pick one. Fortunately, I don't have to pick my way through the thorny problem of which should be first. My uncle wants the daughter I don't choose to marry his neighbour to maintain the peace between them. He is a Christian who will only take one wife and neither of my cousins wants him.'

'Why not?'

'Because you people, you infidel, you don't bathe, so to us you stink. My cousins are adamant they would rather die than be married to such a man, hence my dilemma.'

'We smell?' Galen said, surprised.

'A lot,' Hatim said. 'It amuses me you ignored the rest of my tale and all my woes, but this one comment about personal hygiene fascinates you. I also wonder what on earth possessed me to tell you any of this? Maybe your unprepossessing nature invites confidences. Whatever it is, we have a language lesson to get on with and as the sun has returned, we have some decent light to work with again too.'

At his words and a flick of his head at the door, a slave hurried to open it and a wave of cool air rolled in. Outside, it was already growing brighter as the clouds dispersed and the birdsong returned. First just the occasional cheep, but that quickly built till it sounded like the courtyard was filled to overflowing with birds.

'Now, to work,' Hatim said. 'Show me the original alphabet of your language.'

'Very well,' Galen said and took his first proper look at the writing implements that had been laid down before him. The ink was immediately recognisable, but the quill looked strange because it was a darker brown than he expected and weighed more, too.

As he lifted it up to eye level, Hatim said, 'It's made from a reed. It will last longer and need less trimming than a quill made from a feather.'

'I see.'

Galen dipped the pen into the ink and smoothed the page before he produced the first line of the first rune. It felt different, coarser than parchment and as he drew his line the ink soaked into the page in a way he'd never seen before and, where the ink had been heaviest, it seeped outwards like dye into cloth.

'Oh!'

'It's paper,' Hatim said. 'I assume since your books are vellum, you haven't come across paper before.'

'What is it made from?'

'Old rags mostly,' Hatim said. 'We have a burgeoning cloth trade with cotton and linen coming from all the great centres of the Dar al-Islam. Once the cloth gets too old and threadbare to wear, it is torn into shreds and made into paper.'

'Fascinating,' Galen said as he leaned close to the paper to examine it.

It was indeed made of minute fibres all melded together. He'd think about that later. For now, he had another task. Galen was glad he had something easy to start with as he explained runes and the sounds associated with them.

He linked them to the Latin alphabet, and it impressed him how quickly Hatim picked everything up. So he was clever as well. Galen shouldn't have been surprised by that since Hatim had trained as a doctor.

'I see,' Hatim said as they reached the end of the alphabet. 'Now I can teach you my alphabet. You will see it is vastly superior. But first I need to explain that our script goes from right to left, and we don't use vowels. Also, all our letters are linked in a cursive script, with gaps between the words.'

'Ahhh,' Galen said and glanced up at Jariya, who had continued to write all the way through the lesson, although she surely didn't understand a word they had said.

It was only now, as he watched her properly, that Galen realised she was indeed writing from right to left.

'Focus,' Hatim said, tapping his pen on the paper.

It wasn't as easy for Galen to understand Hatim's explanation of his alphabet as it had been for Hatim to understand the runes. Maybe because Galen had no common frame of reference. Or maybe because he was growing tired and his head was swimming. He wished to stop, or at least plead for a rest, but he didn't dare.

Galen was saved from further lectures as a portly man, dressed as richly as Hatim but with far more rings on his fingers, appeared in the archway to the garden. He spoke to Hatim, sounding peeved. His already red face, glistening with sweat under a beard and a turban, grew steadily redder.

The angelic-looking guard crossed the room and barred the man from entering. Galen had never heard the guard speak before and was surprised by the high, childlike voice that issued from his throat. But there was also no disguising his authority when he prevented the man as he tried to reach for A'isha's arm.

Hatim put his pen down with slow determination and took his time getting to his feet. It was a show of power, making the other man wait. All the while, the guard kept the loud man from entering. Finally Hatim was beside the guard and spoke in a low voice that conveyed that he was calm and dangerous to cross.

Galen was fascinated by the fact that he could understand intent even though he couldn't speak a word of Arabic. He wasn't surprised when the chubby man flounced off, still looking aggrieved.

'That was one of my uncles. He's the youngest half-brother to my father and the amir. He wants to marry A'isha, which is why Aleko stopped him.'

'The angelic man?' Galen asked. It was the first time he'd heard his name. 'He has the voice of a child.'

Hatim laughed and said, 'That's because he's a eunuch. He's a Saqaliba, a pagan Slav captured at a young age and castrated so he could become a guard for a harem. Slavs make some of the best eunuchs. Them and the Turks.'

'You have eunuchs guarding the women?'

'Who else would you use? It's safer for all concerned to have outsiders with no political ambitions looking after the women. But we also need men who cannot procreate, just to be on the safe side. Don't let his effeminate voice and appearance fool you, Aleko is one of the best swordsmen in my uncle's palace.'

'There are so many differences,' Galen murmured.

'Do your women folk mix freely with the men? It wasn't the case even for my mother growing up.'

'Not entirely. Women roam about freely during the day. But at night, they would often retire to the women's room. They kept themselves safe by being together, and the female slaves and servants slept with them, adding to their protection.'

'So you see, not so different.'

Galen wasn't convinced. While it sounded the same on the surface, he felt it was more different than Hatim assumed. He said no more on the subject however, mainly because he didn't have the courage, but also because he was feeling light-headed. His pain was growing and all he wanted to do was rest his head on the pillow.

Chapter 9

It had taken Alcuin a while to get used to drawing on paper. His paints soaked in more deeply and colours would bleed into each other. It was annoying, but at the same time produced colour effects he'd never seen before that intrigued him. So he spent some time creating simple patterns that tested these new qualities. Fortunately, the man who came each day to bring them food and replenish his art supplies seemed not to mind that Alcuin was using up as much paint and paper as he was.

He'd had this mysterious new medium explained to him by Hatim, who'd come by to inspect the bishop's latest injury. Sigburt had given him as hard a time as usual and tried to keep his injured hand away. Hatim wouldn't hear of it though, and had a couple of guards hold the bishop down while he tended to the grisly wound.

Despite the bishop's woes, Alcuin was relieved to be out of the permanent dark of the cell and happy to have something to occupy his mind. Sigburt seemed not to care. Alcuin suspected he was in too much pain to do more than allow Alcuin to raise him from his curled up huddle in the corner to feed him.

Even the food had improved. They were given a porridge with their dry bread, and an extra bowl of water. They needed that. It got hot in their little room. Possibly because they were up high and, Alcuin assumed, right under the roof. Aside from one morning of an astonishingly heavy downpour, it seemed the sun always shone in this land.

Now that he could distinguish night from day, Alcuin had also taken to marking the passage of time in short, neat bundles of black lines on one of his sheets of paper. So far, he'd spent two whole weeks in this new prison with not a single word about Galen. He was beginning to fear that he and his friend would never be reunited.

'You, artist,' Hatim said one afternoon shortly after the bishop had been returned to their cell. 'Come with me if you wish to see your friend.'

'Galen? You're letting me see Galen?'

'He has been asking after you. You should be grateful I am doing this. I am merely here to inform you of this fact, since I'm the only one who can speak Latin around here.'

'Surely you have more Latin speakers,' Alcuin said, and he had to break into a trot to keep up with Hatim, who was trailing a pair of slaves as well as a couple of guards.

'We have a few translators, but they are used to working on the written word. They also say your Latin sounds strange to them. I have to say it sounds odd to me too. Your pronunciation of words differs from what I'm used to.'

'Yes, we had similar difficulties understanding the Latin of the Frankish monks who came to visit our abbey,' Alcuin said as he followed Hatim down the narrow staircase, along the open-sided corridor, the opposite side of which he could see from his cell window, and down a second wider flight of stairs.

They crossed the courtyard Alcuin usually looked down upon and a wonderful scent wafted from the dark, leathery green leaves of the trees that ringed the space. Upon closer inspection as they passed by, Alcuin spotted tiny greenish-white flowers. Was it possible that delicious scent could come from such an innocuous bloom? Apparently so. Now wasn't the time to be distracted by that, though.

Alcuin couldn't believe that he was going to see Galen and his mind bristled with suspicion. Why was this visit being allowed? What were the Moors after, and really, why were they working so hard to keep Galen alive?

Well... maybe that one was understandable. Hatim had obviously relished the challenge of healing Galen. He was an interesting case for him, and the Moor would want to continue to observe Galen's progress to see how well his intervention had worked.

This hopefully kept Galen safe for a while yet. Alcuin was far less certain for his own future. Either way, he wouldn't give Galen any cause for concern.

Hatim walked up to a double door and said, 'Enjoy your visit.'

One half of the door was opened, and a guard pushed Alcuin inside. Then they slammed the door shut behind him and a key turned in the lock with a click. Alcuin's first thought was that it was a trap because it was dark.

Then his eyes gradually grew accustomed to the gloom. The size of the room surprised him. It was more like a great hall, except that it was square, there was no central fire pit and instead of wooden walls, he was surrounded by a carved latticework of stone.

Thin shafts of light pierced the darkness from high above. It provided only sufficient light to make out the space and a narrow low bed placed incongruously in the centre of the room. It was dwarfed in the large space.

'Alcuin? Alcuin, is that you?' Galen whispered and his words drifted across to Alcuin with surprising clarity.

'Yes, yes, it's me,' Alcuin said and hurried over, his footsteps sounding loud and hollow on the smooth marble floor. 'It's good to see you again, my friend. Thank God you are still alive. Now lie back on those cushions and don't strain yourself.'

'Oh Alcuin, thank the Lord you're alright!' Galen whispered. 'Are you alright?'

'Of course I am. Why wouldn't I be?'

'I was told that they locked you up... held you prisoner.'

'Just like you.' Noting the panic in Galen's voice, Alcuin forced himself to calm down and revert to his almost disinterested voice that always worked to still Galen's fear. 'This is a strange room. Is this where they have been keeping you?'

'No,' Galen said and placed his hand on Alcuin's arm, as if to touch him brought reassurance. 'I have been in a much smaller room, the place where Hatim performs his surgeries. I don't know why I'm here. They just carried me in and left me.'

'How odd.' Now that his eyes were properly adjusted to the dark, Alcuin could see that, aside from Galen's bed, the room was devoid of furniture. 'Why would they bring you here just for a meeting with me?'

'I don't know,' Galen said and plucked at Alcuin's sleeve. 'Are you sure you're alright? You're not just saying that for my sake? Hatim told me they are torturing Bishop Sigburt.'

'Ah, yes, I'm afraid they are. Their leader, Zayd Al-Ifriqi, is obsessed with finding the second treasure.'

'Oh no!' Galen whispered. 'What are they doing to him?'

Alcuin doubted the wisdom of telling Galen what was actually going on. But, at the same time, his friend's overactive imagination was capable of coming up with something even worse.

'After whipping failed to loosen his tongue, the Moors started by chopping off the fingers of his left hand one at a time. Since that didn't get the secret out of him, they are threatening to chop off what remains of his hand. I fear after that they will start on his right hand.'

Galen blanched and said with more of a tremor to his voice, 'Why doesn't he just tell them where the second treasure is?'

'Your guess is as good as mine,' Alcuin said with a sigh and knelt down so that he was closer to Galen.

'Whatever Sigburt's reason, he is staunch in his refusal to reveal anything.'

'Why would he refuse? They showed me the first treasure. It is wonderful indeed. I can't see how a second one could be better. So why hide it?'

'I wish I knew. Perhaps it's still on the boat.'

Alcuin took another look around the room as he spoke. There was something odd about it and the way their words magnified and travelled to every corner.

'But Sigburt has not said that the treasure was washed overboard,' Galen said. 'Or so I've been told.'

'Sigburt didn't tell me that, but the less I know, the less I can tell the Moors,' Alcuin said, keeping quiet about what Hatim had said about betraying the bishop and discovering what the second treasure was.

'But you don't remember a second treasure on the boat, do you?'

'Do you?'

'I barely recall being on the beach. It has a hazy quality to it, like a dream.'

'I'm not surprised. You were running a fever.'

'But, Alcuin,' Galen said, his grip tightening on his friend's sleeve and an unaccustomed smile spreading across his face, 'I had a vision! I've never had a vision before, but when I was lying on the sand, I saw a great golden cross glowing in the sunshine. It was a sign from God.'

This tale from the usually level-headed Galen surprised Alcuin. His friend was more likely to ascribe the fantastical to some everyday reason than to a miracle. More so now that people were calling him a saint. For a moment, he wondered whether he should keep his suspicion to himself, but that would be to lie to his friend.

'I'm sorry, Galen, but that was no vision. You told the Moors not to kill the sailors and in return you told them of the bishop's treasure chest, and that's where they found his golden cross.'

'It wasn't a vision?' Galen sounded so disappointed that Alcuin felt a need to apologise. 'It was that cross?'

'I'm afraid so. But you were delirious at the time, so that's probably why it has a dreamlike quality to you.'

'Ah,' Galen murmured, 'so the cross was the first treasure, the one Hatim showed me, and the second treasure remains a mystery.'

'Apparently so.'

A faint rustle, like silk rubbing across silk, distracted Alcuin. It sounded like it was in the room with him and Galen. How could that be?

It was surely his overwrought nerves playing tricks on him and making sounds from outside seem louder. Then again, it was next to impossible to hear anything else over his and Galen's whispering. Even the ever-present birdsong was damped so much it could hardly be heard.

'And aside from the cross, there were only silver coins in the chest,' Galen said.

'Do you think you can work out where the second treasure is?' Alcuin asked because he had more faith in Galen's reasoning ability than his friend had in himself. 'If anyone can do it, it's you.'

Galen gave him a slight smile but said, 'I don't know. Maybe it really was washed overboard.'

'If it was, then why doesn't the bishop say so?'

'Maybe he's playing for time. Maybe he fears what might happen once the Moors no longer need us.'

Alcuin had a similar fear and wasn't cheered that Galen had come to the same conclusion.

'Maybe it's very small,' Galen said. 'Maybe it's amongst the bags of silver coins or on the bishop's person.'

'They've searched us all, removed all the rings from the bishop's fingers and his gold brooch, and yet he holds fast to the fact that they don't have the second treasure.'

Galen's frown deepened and his head twitched as he considered the problem.

Alcuin didn't want him to strain himself too much and bring on a fever. He pressed the back of his hand to Galen's temple and was relieved to feel that he was fine, neither too hot nor too cold.

'Never mind the treasure for the moment. Tell me how you are doing. Are they treating you well?'

'I'm fine.'

'No really, Galen, tell me. I was present when Hatim performed his surgery and I feared he was adding to your woes. I felt just as helpless as I did with the leech Irminric and I couldn't do a thing to stop him.'

Galen plucked restlessly at his blanket and said, 'I'm a little better, actually. I'm very weak still, but I haven't felt cold since I woke up. That could be because it is so hot here, but it is a relief.'

'And the pain?'

'I still have the pain, but I think... I'm not sure, but I think it is less than it was. I feel better than I felt after Ivetta treated me.'

'Thank God, I was very worried for you, but you continue to cheat death.'

'Do I?'

'We were washed overboard. We would surely have drowned. Then you were bleeding, and they threw you up onto their horse and rode hard. By the time we got here you had lost so much blood I was certain you would die.'

'What are you saying?'

'Despite your suffering I feel... well, God is looking out for you, isn't he?'

'For us. You also didn't drown.'

'Maybe only because I was with you.'

'Alcuin, don't.'

'Alright, I know how you dislike it, but still, it is remarkable,' Alcuin said and glanced around the room again. He had a prickling sensation run up and down his spine that they were being watched. It really was best to keep from saying anything that would bring them more danger.

Galen nodded, watching Alcuin's face as thoughts chased across his own. He was perceptive, and no doubt had picked up on Alcuin's unease. But he was sensible enough not to say anything and then his face took on a more faraway expression.

'Maybe the second treasure isn't made from gold or silver,' Galen said, mulling over his latest idea.

'Not made from gold? What are you talking about?'

'The Moors have taken everything of value from us and yet the bishop's actions imply that he still has the treasure.'

'But what could it be, then? What could be more precious than gold?'

'Books?'

Galen looked amused at what Alcuin assumed was his own astonished face.

'We don't have books either, not anything of great value at any rate, just your two codices.'

'No, but between the two of us, we have the makings of as many fine books as you could ever wish to lay your hands upon.'

The idea was astonishing, but Alcuin felt it had a ring of truth to it.

'We're the second treasure? Could that be true? Impossible! Besides, what was the bishop going to do? Hand us over to the pope as a gift to be chained to a couple of desks somewhere in the Vatican and produce manuscripts until we died?'

Galen gave a big, expressive shrug. He looked tired now, worn down by this brief visit and his own deep thoughts.

'Maybe. Bishop Sigburt has ever had his own interests foremost in his heart. Would he care how we felt to be left behind if it got him what he desired?'

'He's ambitious enough to want to be the pope.'

'Once he was in Rome, he could even have worked towards that,' Galen said. 'But only if he is in Rome, and not if he is chopped into little pieces.'

'He's already speaking of being martyred.'

Galen shuddered at the idea.

'That is the next best thing to being a pope, I suppose.'

'That or a saint.'

Alcuin wished he hadn't said anything as Galen gave him an alarmed look. He also worried about potential eavesdroppers. Although, there was nobody here who could understand them when they spoke Englisc, so hopefully that kept them safe. Either way, Alcuin decided not to say anything of the bishop's desire for him to get Galen to Rome, be he alive or dead.

'Never mind that for the moment. Tell me instead if the Moors are treating you well. You haven't said.'

'I am fine. I am fed and kept in bed to heal. No need to worry about me.'

'Except that you are surrounded by strangers.'

Alcuin wasn't going to tell Galen that he already knew what an ordeal he was going through, but he hoped his friend might unburden himself given the chance.

'You know I am uncomfortable around strangers and... and I don't have my clothes and–' Galen stopped, gave a quick embarrassed smile and said, 'I really have nothing to complain about. Yours and Bishop Sigburt's positions are far worse.'

'Aside from the torture, we are also being treated well. The bishop's wounds are taken care of and we are both fed and the cell is comfortable enough.'

'Do you think we will ever be set free?' Galen asked wistfully.

'I don't know. I can't see what they might want to do with us, really. Although they could just decide to kill us,' Alcuin said, and then regretted it as he saw Galen's eyes flicker in fright. 'Maybe they'll just be tempted to ransom us.'

'They wouldn't get much for me.'

'Me neither,' Alcuin said with a laugh. 'Best we don't tell the Moors, though.'

Galen sighed and said, 'I'd hoped to see my mother again and now it's looking less and less likely.'

'Don't give up yet. I have faith that things will work out alright for the two of us.'

Chapter 10

Galen had spoken the truth when he told Alcuin that he was feeling better. In fact, these days, aside from the lethargy which clung to his body and made every movement a tremendous effort, he couldn't remember feeling this well since the day he'd woken up in his uncle's infirmary in the abbey after he' saved his life. Whatever Hatim had done was far better than anything anyone else had ever managed.

Meeting with Alcuin had also been a profound relief. To see his smiling, familiar face in this place had made hope seem possible. Of course, the moment Alcuin had been taken away and Galen's bed carried back into this room, he started to worry again.

The meeting, in particular seemed, odd. It made Galen play the conversation over and over in his mind. He checked and re-checked what had been said and wondered whether any of it might damn them later. He prayed to God that it wouldn't.

That was ever his burden: to worry on and on about things he couldn't change. Still, there was a chink of light and maybe more than that. If he could find the second treasure, then he would hand it over if he could. He didn't care how holy it was or how angry it made Bishop Sigburt, as long as it bought their freedom.

Now there was a thought: freedom. Galen was desperate to go back home and worried that he might never be allowed to. The Moors had so many slaves and he suspected that he and Alcuin might soon join their ranks. That was assuming they did not kill them for being holy men.

Galen feared both options and wondered whether it would be possible to negotiate their release. For that, he'd need a strong bargaining chip. Possibly, only the whereabouts of the second treasure would give them enough leverage.

The sound of approaching footsteps pulled him from considering his future. Since it was the time Hatim usually appeared, it didn't surprise Galen to see him or his entourage. Today, though, aside from laying out the usual writing implements, one slave placed a bright round orange object on a plate beside the thin morning broth.

The slave knelt down, took a wickedly sharp knife from his belt and cut into what Galen assumed was some kind of fruit. It released a fine spray with a pungent, unfamiliar, sweet and sour aroma as the slave peeled away a thick section of skin. Under the skin, the fruit was divided into segments that the slave pulled apart, one by one, and placed in a row on the plate.

'What is it?'

'It's an orange,' Hatim said. 'You are fortunate to be able to try one. These are the last few remaining after the winter crop and were stored in our ice house.'

'An ice house?'

'A half-buried building filled with ice carried down from the mountain. It's where we keep food fresh for longer. Oranges being a case in point. It is a shame that this is all the fresh fruit I can give you for now. Al-Andalus has a great wealth of fruits, vegetables and grains that I am certain you have never come across before. However, you will soon discover all the delights this land of plenty has to offer as we are approaching summer.'

The way Hatim spoke confirmed Galen's worst fears. The Moor, at least, had no intention of letting them go.

'Try the orange,' Hatim said, waving both hands encouragingly. 'You will like it.'

'But why are you giving me such a delicacy?'

'You are much improved. Until now, I didn't want to give you too much to eat, so as to give my stitches a chance to heal your body. Now we can gradually build you up to full strength and for that, you must eat more. Not too much more though, just fruit and porridge for the time being.'

Hearing that Hatim thought he was on the mend considerably cheered Galen and he reached for a segment of orange with more than his usual enthusiasm. Until his illness, that had robbed him of the desire to eat, Galen had never been a picky eater. He usually found new experiences intriguing rather than alarming. Since Hatim looked so enthusiastic, it must surely be alright.

Galen bit down on the fruit and felt a slight popping sensation, then his nostrils filled with the intense aroma of the orange and his mouth watered as the acidic and sweet flavour of the fruit enveloped his tongue.

'Well?' Hatim said as he settled on his cushion. 'It's good, isn't it?'

'Delicious,' Galen said, his mouth full.

'Eat it all. It's a rare treat at this time of year, but good for you.'

Galen didn't need further encouragement, but he felt bad for the slave who had peeled the orange. The man watched every segment as it travelled from the plate into Galen's mouth and at one point, he even sucked in his lips and swallowed.

Since Galen could do nothing for the man, he turned to Jariya, who was taking notes as usual, and then A'isha, who was playing her lute. Eating oranges obviously held less interest for them, probably because they could eat them whenever they felt like it.

'Now, are you ready for your lesson?' Hatim asked.

Galen hadn't finished the orange yet. It was on the large side, but he was eager to return to learning Arabic so pushed his plate aside.

'I am, but... can I ask you about yesterday?'

Hatim tilted his head as if he were listening, but his expression hardened.

'What about it?'

Galen was always wary of confronting powerful men and Hatim was no exception, but he still needed to know.

'I am grateful, of course. I have been worrying about Alcuin, but it just seemed... strange. Why yesterday, and why in that dark room?'

'My uncle commanded it and I have no reason to question him.'

Hatim spoke brusquely, which was enough to prevent Galen from asking more.

Since he could go no further in that direction, Galen said, 'I... I noticed that Alcuin smelled. I mean... he has always smelled of himself, but it seemed to be more intense yesterday.'

Hatim laughed and said, 'You see? Now that you have bathed regularly, you understand what I mean about the smell. You are all like that, even your bishop stinks. Do you not have public baths in your land?'

'Public what?' Galen said, back to being confused.

'A place where the entire population can go to get clean.'

'We have rivers.' Galen suspected that wasn't what Hatim was referring to. 'And at the abbey we wash our hands before prayer in a communal trough.'

'What about the rest? How often do you bathe?'

'Once a year, at Easter.'

'Once a year!' Hatim looked profoundly shocked and then broke into Arabic to inform everyone else in the room of this newly learned fact.

Galen felt himself colour all the way to the tips of his ears at the gasps, tuts and horrified looks this information engendered. Jariya shook her head and A'isha actually covered her mouth with her veil, as if he was even now polluting their air.

'How astonishing. I can't even comprehend cleaning so little. I'm amazed anyone is still alive in your kingdom. Although I admit, most of the people of Christendom seem to have a similar lack of hygiene,' Hatim said. 'One day soon, when you are stronger, I will take you to have a proper bath. None of this washing you down with a sponge.'

Galen shuddered at the idea but thought it best not to say anything against the proposal. At least now he had the distraction of study. He was finding learning a new language a satisfying challenge.

Hatim seemed to enjoy the process just as much as Galen and the sun was considerably higher in the sky when he said, 'That's enough for today. I do have one question before we stop, though.'

'What is it?'

Galen was always wary of Hatim for he never knew why any particular question was asked in the first place. Still, he composed his face into a query and waited.

'I saw what I took to be poems in your notebook, but as they are in Englisc, I wasn't sure.'

'Oh. Some of them are poems, yes.'

'Written by you?'

Galen was surprised by how Hatim perked up and looked impressed, and he blushed so much his face felt hot.

'Not all of them. Some are poems and riddles that I just liked.'

'But you wrote some of them yourself,' Hatim pressed.

'Is that a good thing?'

'My people value poets very highly. A man demonstrates his wit by composing poems. The most entertaining times I've had were when groups of men compete against each other, making up poems, each trying to outdo the rest.'

'Do you take part?'

'Not only do I take part, I win. My uncle was so impressed with my prowess that he made me his heir because of this ability.'

'Poetry is that important?'

Galen could hardly imagine a similar thing happening in a long hall. Sure, men who could sing or tell a good riddle or tale were popular. But they were judged on their ability as warriors and managers of their land.

'Knowledge is important,' Hatim said. 'All knowledge. I am also renowned for having memorised the Qur'an and for becoming a surgeon. It is no small feat.'

'That is true.'

'Will you tell me one of your poems?' Hatim said, flicking Galen's book open and pointing at a block of text. 'How about this one?'

'That's a riddle,' Galen said. 'I'll have to translate it into Latin for you, so you won't get the full enjoyment from it. My people are very keen on alliteration.'

'Yes, so I see, the repetition of the same sound is evident, on word after word. No matter. Translate it into the Latin and I will demonstrate my wisdom by solving it.'

Galen had no choice but to comply, but he worried about what might happen if Hatim failed to solve the puzzle.

'They are fiendishly difficult,' Galen said, with little hope of being listened to.

'Go ahead,' Hatim said, waving his hand nonchalantly. He then said something to his entourage, and they all looked impressed, too. It seemed poets really were revered here.

'Well... alright, here goes,' Galen said and translated as his finger moved along the line of text.

'I am a lofty thing known to all, the highborn, the mighty and the lowly.

I travel widely from farm to ham to burh.

I have success and bright reward in cities.

Wise men love my presence.

To many, I will declare wisdom.

Though now the sons of men eagerly seek the tracks I make,
I sometimes conceal my paths from all mankind.
At first a stranger, the delight of plunderers.
Once you know me, we shall endure, friends till the last.'

Galen stopped and looked expectantly at Hatim.

'Is that it?' Hatim asked.

Galen was surprised.

'Have you worked it out already?'

'Ha!' Hatim said. 'It is trickier than I expected. Are you sure your translation is up to scratch?'

'It is accurate,' Galen said, not wishing to start an argument or offend his captor. 'Do you want me to repeat it?'

'Yes, do that. Go slower this time.'

So Galen repeated the riddle, going line by line.

'We expect the riddles to keep people guessing and entertained for the whole evening. If it was too easy, it would be over in the blink of an eye.'

'Yes, I can see that. Is that why it is so deliberately obtuse? Give it to me again. This time I will also translate it for everybody else.'

So Galen repeated the riddle for a third time, waiting as Hatim translated everything into Arabic. Jariya wrote it down and then laid the book open on the table beside Galen's while she, A'isha and Hatim pored over the script and debated amongst themselves, with the slaves and Aleko making occasional suggestions. Thankfully, everyone seemed to be enjoying themselves.

Galen took the time while they were arguing to try and read Jariya's translation, slowly sounding out the letters. It was strange to see his riddle in this foreign tongue.

'This is tricky indeed,' Hatim said after what felt like such a long period of chatter that Galen's reserves grew depleted and he leaned back on his cushions. 'The thing you describe is known to all men and is found in all the places of man. It is loved by the wise, but for some reason, it sometimes hides itself. It is a curious thing indeed.'

'Do you give up?' Galen asked, hopeful that everyone would leave him to get some sleep.

Hatim shook his head and went back to debating the riddle and Galen watched the conversation. A'isha, as expected, was boisterous and cheerfully throwing out suggestions one after the other. They elicited a lot of laughter, but whenever Hatim asked Galen if her guesses were right, he shook his head.

Jariya was altogether more thoughtful. She nibbled on the end of her pen as she ran a finger along each line of text, considering. After a while, her eyebrows rose and she spoke.

'Jariya suggests it's the moon,' Hatim said.

'That's a good guess,' Galen said, surprised that the young woman had considered it so deeply. 'The moon is certainly lofty, known to all and travels a great deal. You must know that sometimes our Anglo-Saxon riddles refer to more than one thing. It's a trick to throw people off the track. The moon is one possible solution, but it isn't the main solution.'

'Then, my friend, you will have to give us the answer, for our prayer time beckons and you look like you need a rest. So tell me, what is the answer?'

'It's a riddle,' Galen said, touched and surprised that Hatim had called him a friend, even if it was unthinking.

'I know it's a riddle,' Hatim said, speaking now as he would to an imbecilic child. 'But what is it referring to?'

'Riddles,' Galen said and hurried on. 'The answer is: a riddle. That's why wise men like it, but it is sometimes hidden, but once you know the answer, you're unlikely to forget it.'

Hatim looked astonished for a moment, then gave a loud 'Ha!' and burst out laughing.

Everyone else watched him in surprise and then started calling out in unison for the answer to the riddle. They were equally astonished and also started laughing as he explained it to them.

'Poetry and riddles,' Hatim said, smiling down at Galen. 'Perhaps you will have a worth for my uncle after all. I have been searching for one. Now you must sleep.' Hatim gave Galen a slight nod and ordered everybody out of the room.

Chapter 11

Over the next few days, Galen started to feel considerably better. The fog that had filled his mind for so long lifted and he thanked God for it in his daily prayers. This improvement, plus the long hours he was left alone, gave him a chance to consider his future.

He feared the outlook was bleak — slavery at best. If he were to have any chance of seeing his family again, escape would be his and Alcuin's only option. He worried more about Alcuin than himself because Hatim was so hard to draw on the subject.

Although his throwaway remark after they'd spoken about riddles gnawed at Galen's mind. Why was it essential to prove to his uncle, the amir, that Galen was useful? Was it because people with no use were executed?

Despite his fears, Galen avoided asking about that and about the bishop. If Sigburt were to survive, he'd have to escape too. But Galen feared the old man must be in worse shape than he was and it would be difficult to flee with two invalids. It made the whole enterprise seem like nothing more than a dream.

Then again, Galen had always been a dreamer. His sisters teased him about it, for they and his mother were the only ones who knew how fanciful Galen could be. Best not to think about his mother, really, although she was the spur that got Galen out of bed and working to build his strength.

Galen was familiar now with the daily routine surrounding him. He used the couple of hours after dawn to walk up and down the room. It still hurt to walk, but the pain was less intense and only shot through his body if he put a foot down too hard. He tried his best not to do so, which was made easier by the smooth marble floors.

Occasionally, very early, Galen ventured out into the courtyard. At this hour of the morning, the only sound was the dawn chorus. Later, the sounds of people moving around, chatting, laughing, giving orders and sometimes even arguing, wafted down from the upper balconies. At those times Galen didn't dare leave Hatim's surgery for fear of running into somebody.

But in the cool early morning he'd risked walking all the way out to the central fountain, a deep bowl resting on the backs of four fearsomely scowling lions. Galen had dipped his fingers into the water, further disturbing the reflection of the early morning lavender-tinted sky, and then sucked the moisture from his fingertips. The water was sweet.

He could see why it attracted so many birds who swooped down during the day to take elegant little sips. He was less fond of the intimidating peacocks who would shriek their displeasure at him if he was blocking their access to the fountain. They were beautiful but grumpy birds.

It was also at dawn that Galen heard the first of the day's now-familiar musical cry of the muezzins ringing out across the land. Some sounded close by, others far more distant. Hatim had told him it was their preachers calling everyone to prayer, something the devout did five times a day.

It was the moment Galen returned to the surgery. Even though that was when everyone, from the amir to the lowliest slaves, was engaged in prayer and therefore unlikely to see him. He feared what might happen if he was discovered strolling around the grounds at that sacred time.

Instead, Galen spent the time seated on his bed, deep in his own prayers. After that, he got his books ready and waited for Hatim to start their morning lessons.

Today he was later than usual and Galen wondered why. Thus far, Hatim had always arrived straight after prayers. But Galen had heard life returning to the corridors and balconies of the palace and Hatim didn't appear.

This set Galen to worrying. Any change in routine made him anxious about what it meant. So it was a considerable relief when Hatim arrived, looking no different to any other day, trailing slaves and his cousins all laden with goods.

Before he could stop himself, Galen said, 'Do you ever carry anything for yourself?'

'Why would I?' Hatim said in surprise.

Galen was relieved that Hatim hadn't taken offence at his foolishly spontaneous question. Perhaps their prolonged exposure to each other was having a beneficial effect. Galen no longer felt the terror he had upon seeing Hatim and his entourage. He wondered whether perhaps he had risen in Hatim's estimation from curiosity to something more, as well.

'I don't suppose there is any need for you to carry anything, no.'

Hatim kept his eagle-like gaze on Galen as he settled on the cushion at the other side of the table. There it was again, Galen thought, that curious, searching expression of Hatim weighing him up. No, they weren't friends yet and perhaps they never would be. There was always a barrier between the two of them. It was inevitable when one was a prisoner and the other the captor.

Their lesson was shorter today, which Galen regretted because he was getting the hang of the language now that he'd mastered the letters and learned how to write some basic words. It was no matter, since he had studied on his own in the afternoons when Hatim was never around.

But today, in yet another change, Hatim said, as he stood to take his leave, 'My uncle has been called to Córdoba by the khalifa, Al Mansur. I was seeing him off this morning, which is why I was late.'

'The khalifa?' Galen said. 'Is that your king?'

'I suppose you could call him that.'

'So your uncle, the amir... what is that?'

'An amir is something like a general or a governor. Their role is within the gift of the khalifa. He can give you territory to manage for him, but he can also take it away. Although my family has held this northern territory for a long time.'

'It sounds like the ealdormen of my home. The king gifted their territories to them, but several generations ago. They would fight to hold on to the land should the king ever try to depose them.'

'And your father?'

Galen hesitated, wondering whether he should reveal he was of noble stock and whether it would benefit his current situation or disadvantage it. Overall, he decided it would be an advantage.

'I am the youngest son of an ealdorman.'

Galen watched Hatim closely to judge the effect of his words. Hatim was far too experienced at courtly intrigue to show much emotion, but Galen felt like this admission was less impressive to Hatim than his discovered ability as a scribe and poet.

'Do you think we might try to ransom you?'

'As I said, I'm the youngest son. I doubt you'd get much for me.'

'It is unlikely that my uncle would try,' Hatim said, but for a moment he looked sympathetic. 'Since my uncle is away, he won't need me this afternoon. So after prayers and lunch I shall return and take you and your friend, Alcuin, for a bath.'

'With Alcuin?' Galen said, trying not to make his relief and joy too obvious.

'You have been wondering about him, have you not?'

Galen couldn't deny it, but he wondered why it was happening now, on the very day that the amir left his city. Was Hatim more wary of his uncle than he usually showed?

'And... why a bath?'

Communal bathing sounded dreadful to Galen. He also had strong reservations about the wisdom of regular bathing, no matter what Hatim had to say on the subject. On the other hand, he would see Alcuin.

'This will be good for you on two fronts. You will get clean, and your friend will get clean. Aside from that, you will get a bit of exercise. It is time you started walking.'

'Really, a walk?'

Galen kept to himself that he'd already been trying to do that. As always, he wasn't sure whether it was good or bad that Hatim thought he was improving. Would he be thrown in jail, or subjected to torture once he was fully recovered? Galen had never had the courage to ask, although the limbo of ignorance was painful.

'On our way to the bath, I'll show you a bit of this land in which you now live.'

Now this was good news, so Galen didn't object. He had many reasons not to. First, he didn't dare to. Second, he'd be ignored. Third, he was curious to see more of this place. It was the largest and grandest building he'd ever seen in his life. Finally, he felt he should get a sense of where they were so he could prepare an escape.

The last thought nearly made him laugh. But ever since Septimus attacked him, and after being besieged by vikings, he'd started keeping an eye open for escape routes, no matter how improbable they might be.

'I will see you later,' Hatim said. He gave a nod of farewell and left, his entourage trailing after him.

CHAPTER 12

Galen had just finished eating lunch: a pale, almost white, goat's cheese and dried figs. He rather liked figs. They were soft, intensely sweet, and chewy.

The sound of approaching people reminded him that Hatim was on his way back, and that he'd soon see Alcuin, so he looked up from his bed with more than his usual enthusiasm. Alcuin's appearance shocked him. He hadn't seen him clearly in the gloom of the room where they'd last met but now he looked tired, unshaven and dishevelled.

'Alcuin, are you alright?'

'Happier for seeing you. You're looking a lot better.'

'You aren't, what has happened to you?' Galen said, throwing aside all care for himself or fear of offending their captors.

'I'm just tired. I've been tending to Bishop Sigburt and he is ailing.'

'How bad is he?'

Alcuin shook his head, indicating that the outlook wasn't good.

Galen wanted to know everything, but he was acutely aware that Hatim was watching. This was the first time the Moor was seeing them together. Galen worried about making it too obvious how much he cared for Alcuin lest it be used against him later. He was also more aware than usual of how worried Alcuin looked for him, which was equally dangerous.

'As you have eaten, Brother Galen,' Hatim said, 'shall we try walking? And the two of you must speak Latin whilst in my company.'

'Oh yes, of course,' Galen said and eased himself out of bed.

As his feet were about to touch the ground, Jariya handed a pair of tan and dark brown embossed slippers to Alcuin and showed with a tilt of her chin that he should help put them on Galen.

'Oh yes, of course,' Alcuin said, 'good idea.'

'The floors are so fine and smooth here, I doubt I need shoes,' Galen said.

'Maybe not, but you might offend our hosts if you don't wear them,' Alcuin said as he slipped them onto Galen's feet.

Galen's eyes widened in surprise.

'They are so soft! Like nothing I've ever worn before.'

'Looks to me like they are made from kid leather.'

'They are,' Hatim said, looking amused by the monk's astonishment at something he obviously took as commonplace. 'Now, see if you can stand up.'

Alcuin took a firm hold of Galen's elbow and, in a practised move, helped him to his feet. Since Galen had been practising walking on his own he didn't need the support. Although, with the audience, he was grateful for it. He gave a relieved sigh as he straightened up and slowly looked around. Everyone in the room was watching him, which made him blush, and his gaze dropped to the floor.

'How do you feel?' Alcuin asked.

‘Fine. I feel fine,’ Galen said a little shakily.

‘You’re standing a little more upright than you used to.’

‘It hurts a bit less.’

‘But it still hurts?’ Hatim asked.

‘Just a little.’

Hatim gave a brief nod, but didn’t look convinced that Galen was telling the truth.

‘I don’t know you well, but I have already learned that you don’t like to be a nuisance. You are bound to underplay your discomfort, but that won’t disguise it from me. I merely have to observe how a person carries himself to get an accurate picture of my patient’s condition.’

‘I see,’ Galen said, feeling steadily more embarrassed.

‘Well, let’s go out then, shall we? We will walk to the bathhouse and back. That will provide you with more than enough exercise for today.’

Hatim strolled out into the courtyard and the rest of his party surrounded Alcuin and Galen and moved in a huddle behind him.

‘Lean on me,’ Alcuin said and took a firm grasp of Galen’s arm.

Hatim led his little group through the courtyard, past the fountain splashing out water that ran over the lip of a central bowl and drained away along four channels which divided the courtyard into quarters.

‘It’s a wondrous palace,’ Galen said. ‘And the sun is so bright. Have you ever seen anything like it, Alcuin?’

‘Nothing at all,’ Alcuin said, his eyes wide with wonder.

‘It is just one courtyard. There are many more in my uncle’s palace,’ Hatim said as he led them through another wide archway on the opposite side to his surgery.

Galen hadn't dared to come this far in his clandestine walks lest he come across somebody.

'This stone is as white as milk.'

'It's marble,' Hatim said. 'You will see it all around the palace.'

'And it's carved and inlaid with a pattern.'

Galen pulled at Alcuin, forcing him to slow down. He wanted to give his friend an opportunity to examine this fabulous art. It also gave him a chance to catch his breath. He'd thought he was doing fine with his walks, but they had been considerably slower than the ambling stroll Hatim was taking.

'They decorate everything. The floor has a pattern and the walls are covered in glistening enamels.'

'Tiles actually,' Hatim said.

'It's like the entire palace has been illuminated,' Alcuin said.

'I suppose, in a way, it has. Although this place is as nothing compared to the magnificent palace of Córdoba.'

'Really? Then Córdoba must be very fine indeed.'

'It is the greatest city in the world. Within its walls there are seven hundred mosques, sixty palaces and seventy libraries.'

'Seventy libraries,' Galen said, his eyes as wide as plates to hear of such wonders. 'How is such a thing possible?'

'It isn't,' Alcuin said with a laugh, 'he's having you on.'

'I am not,' Hatim said. 'What's more, the largest of those libraries contains six hundred thousand manuscripts, a hundred thousand more manuscripts than there are people in the city.'

'Do you really expect me to believe that any city can hold half a million people? No! It's impossible. How can you feed them all? How can they fit into the space?'

'We have great ingenuity.'

Hatim led them out of the passageway onto a wide terrace and waved his arms to encompass the view. Below them, past the encircling walls of the palace, was the town of Halab, spilling down the side of the mountain. Its numerous stark white walls and red-tiled roofs glowed in the afternoon sun.

'Do you really believe that your land is so great? That it can compare to anything we Moors have done? Water brought in via aqueducts irrigates the land around Córdoba. Armies of men work the fields and ensure that we all have sufficient to eat. That doesn't present any difficulty for us.'

'Six hundred thousand books,' Galen murmured, not even paying attention to the argument going on across him. 'Our monastery only has two hundred books, and that is considered a lot. How I would like to see such a thing!'

'I'm afraid you can't,' Hatim said. 'Al-Mansur is our khalifa now, and he won't allow Christians into Córdoba. Once, it was possible, but not now, not for monks like you. You may have heard that he sacked your sacred shrine of Santiago de Compostela.'

'No, we hadn't heard that,' Alcuin said.

'I doubt it went down well in Rome. I know for certain the local Christian kings will want a war to win back the land. But all I can say is if you Christians think the people want you back, you are mistaken. Their lives are far more comfortable and well-ordered under Moorish rule.'

'No,' Galen said, shaking his head. 'You are invaders, just like the Romans. They didn't last in Engla-Lond and you won't last here, even if your going results in a hundred years of darkness. You won't remain.'

Hatim looked at Galen in astonishment. Galen had spoken without thinking and he realised by the hard gaze that was directed at him that he'd gone too far.

Alcuin was also looking at Galen in surprise. Then he caught Hatim's eye and gave a wry smile.

'He is good at working things out. If I had to take a wager on who was right, Galen or you, I'd have to go with Galen.'

'Well, if I were him,' Hatim said, 'I wouldn't let my uncle hear words like that.'

'Oh no, I won't breathe a word to any others. I'm sorry I said so much. I didn't mean to cause offence.'

Galen's gaze went back to the town beyond the palace walls. It was bigger than Lundenburh, and even the buildings of the commoners looked impressive. Many rose two and sometimes three storeys high. It looked prosperous and well run, a gem for any kingdom and yet, according to Hatim, this wasn't even the greatest city in the land.

'Come, we've paused here long enough,' Hatim said. 'Time to head to the bathhouse. But who knows, if you behave yourself, maybe one day I'll show you my uncle's library. It may not be as large as the library of Córdoba, but it has many more manuscripts than your monastery library.'

With that, he headed along the terrace, the top end of which had a solid brick building with an impressive set of chimneys. White smoke rose into the still air and the smell of roasting meat and baking bread wafted towards them.

'The kitchen.'

Hatim hardly need bother telling them, Galen thought. This palace might be strange, but kitchen seemed to be similar the world over.

'But what are those birds?' Alcuin said, pointing to a gathering of half a dozen large, long-legged, blue-necked, long-tailed brown birds. At that precise moment one of the birds turned towards them, lifted up his tail and spread it like a magnificent green and blue velvet fan.

'It's a peacock,' Galen said, flushing with the pleasure of Alcuin's dazzled astonishment. 'It's quite something isn't it?'

'They gather around the kitchen looking for scraps,' Hatim said.

Galen was thrilled that Alcuin had seen a peacock, but of more interest was that the kitchen were built close to an outer wall. Carts and men laden with goods were flowing through the nearby gate from the city. Galen glanced up at Alcuin and they shared a conspiratorial look. This was an exit.

Then they both looked back to where Hatim was leading them, a garden screened by tall, arrow-shaped dark trees. And Alcuin was apparently reminded of their destination.

'What is a bathhouse?'

Galen smiled at him.

'It's exactly what you suspect.'

The tall dark trees formed a hedge that now blocked Galen's view and he turned to examine the garden he was in. It was a simple place with closely cropped grass in the centre crossed by a brick-paved path. It seemed stark compared to Galen's mother's garden that had always been lush and filled with flowers in the summer. Perhaps the heat was too much for them. Hatim had said outside was warmer, but he'd not realised how much warmer till they were standing in the full glare of the sun.

At the far end of the garden was a squat building made from the same simple brown bricks as the kitchen. A portico at the front was the only ornamentation. That and the narrow windows placed so high nobody could look inside.

A fat old man stood at the entrance and bowed deeply at Hatim's approach.

'This is the palace bath. I have made sure that today nobody but us will be using it.'

'Your cousins?' Galen asked, astonished that the two women had accompanied them this far.

'They will stay outside. Men and women never bathe together. In the city, the bathhouse alternates between days for the men and days for the women and the same is true for the people in the palace. But today I have ordered that I be given a couple of hours just for us.'

'Just for us?'

Galen supposed it was better for the bath to be restricted to only the handful of men currently with them. They had all seen him naked before, not that it made it any easier. But two hours? Surely no bath could take so long?

The fat old man ushered everyone into a plain antechamber with a red brick floor and handed each of them a long white cloth.

'What is this?' Alcuin asked.

'It's to preserve your modesty. When men gather for a bath, we rarely bother with such a thing, but I guessed you and Galen would prefer it, so remove your garments, and wrap that around your waists.'

Galen was surprised that Alcuin looked even less keen to disrobe than he did himself. Alcuin was muttering into his scapular as he pulled it over his head and then dropped it on the floor before removing his tunic. One of the two slaves that always followed Hatim scooped everybody's clothes up off the floor and placed the items into baskets, one per person. Galen assumed that as the slaves weren't also disrobing, they wouldn't be taking a bath.

Galen wrapped the linen cloth about his waist. He'd wait till the last moment before he removed the robe.

Hatim first undid his wide belt, then stepped out of his voluminous trousers and tossed them to the bathhouse attendant. Finally, he pulled off his outer robe, then his inner, till he was standing stark naked in the room, patting his hairy chest in satisfaction. Galen hastily looked away but not before he'd noted the powerful muscles of Hatim's legs, shoulders and arms.

His behaviour might be that of an indolent layabout, but his body spoke of somebody who spent hours in training. Galen supposed that made sense. No man, no matter how learned and good at poetry, would be chosen as the next ruler without also being a powerful warrior.

'Alright, the last bit, Brother Galen,' Hatim said.

Galen reluctantly slipped out of his plain white cotton robe and stood, crouched over, his arms wrapped about his body. He was the smallest, skinniest man there. Alcuin, despite his long imprisonment, was well built and muscular, which made Galen feel even more self-conscious. Not that Alcuin looked comfortable.

'Right, now we will go into the first room.'

Hatim stepped through a pair of doors into a room whose principal feature was a large square brick tub filled with stones. The heat of a fire rose from the stones and Galen stopped, pulling Alcuin, who clung to Galen more than was usual, to a halt.

'Dear God, but it's hot in here.'

'It's the steam room. Sit,' Hatim said, and pointed to a wooden bench along the wall beside the tub of heated stone.

'A steam room?' Alcuin's voice was heavy with suspicion, and he huddled beside Galen, looking about nervously. 'Are we sure this isn't some form of torture?'

'If it was, why would Hatim be with us?'

Hatim took a ladle of water he'd scooped from a bucket and poured it over the stones. The ensuing hiss and billow of steam made Galen jump, and he too wondered whether this was indeed a form of torture.

It seemed not to be as Hatim gave a deep, satisfied sigh and settled on the bench, grinning from ear to ear.

'What is this vision of hell?' Alcuin asked.

'Relax and enjoy the cleansing process of the heat and steam.'

'Cleansing? We're going to be boiled alive.'

'Nonsense. The sweat is the first step to cleanse your body.'

'The first step?' Galen asked because this implied more steps and if they were all as excessive as the first, it was truly going to be a feat of endurance.

'It might seem strange at first,' Hatim said as he leaned his head back against the wall and closed his eyes, 'but believe me, you will grow to enjoy it.'

Galen had his doubts and shared a dubious look with Alcuin, who was still as alarmed as if he was being tortured.

'Maybe we should try to enjoy it,' Galen said, and reflected that it was the hottest he'd ever felt. Like Alcuin, he feared he might be roasted to death in this room. But he couldn't believe that Hatim would look so pleased by the prospect as he appeared to be.

After a while, and several more scoops of water thrown over the rocks, the heat had penetrated through Galen's body. Sweat dripped down his face and off the tip of his nose. It ran in rivulets down his chest and formed puddles about his toes. He had never felt this hot in all his life. But he was growing accustomed to it. He thought that when he'd been suffering from the cold after the leech Irminric's treatment, this steam room would have been very welcome.

'How much longer?'

Alcuin had slumped forward but raised his head as he asked the question.

'Time for the next step,' Hatim said, perhaps prompted by Alcuin's beet-red face. 'Come along.'

Galen and Alcuin were eager to get out of the heat, but nervous about what came next. As it was, they stepped into a blessedly cool space where a deep pool of dark water took up much of the room.

'Come on,' Hatim said, stepping down into the pool, and then wading to the middle, where he submerged himself.

'This is madness,' Alcuin said, standing stock still.

'Think of it like swimming in a river,' Galen said, trying to pull Alcuin back into motion.

'I never swam in the river. I don't like water, not even for drinking.'

It surprised Galen to discover this. He'd thought he knew everything about Alcuin, but this was news to him.

'You don't like water?'

'How can you even ask that after what happened in the sea? I never want to be submerged again.'

'I don't think you have a choice,' Galen said, glancing towards Hatim, who was entertaining himself by sinking beneath the water, coming up again for air, and then sinking once again.

Galen wasn't eager to get into the water, but he was so hot still that everything, his chest, arms and legs, was pink, and Alcuin was the same.

'Galen, we have to escape,' Alcuin whispered, leaning toward his friend's ear. 'This place is dangerous and who knows what they are planning for us?'

'I know,' Galen said and used as much strength as he could to pull Alcuin towards the water. 'But it seems impossible.'

'All the same, we have to try. I have been working on the lock in my cell and it is coming loose. I have also been memorising all the places I see. You must do the same. Try to work out the rhythm of the palace. The more we know, the better.'

Galen nodded, glancing anxiously towards Hatim, who seemed too distracted to hear what they were saying. Galen wasn't sure he trusted what he saw.

'Also,' Alcuin whispered in Englisc but with his eyes fixed on Hatim, or at least where he might emerge, as he was currently back underwater, 'don't get attached to that man. I know what you're like. If anyone shows you an ounce of kindness, you like them back wholeheartedly. That isn't safe here.'

'Yes, yes, I know,' Galen said, glancing back anxiously at Hatim, who came up to the surface in a great burst of bubbles. Then Galen took a first step into the water, pulling his arm out of Alcuin's anxious grip.

The water was chilly. As cold as any river at home. But whereas there, he'd have shuddered to go in, now, hot as he was, the water came as a blessed relief.

'It's nice, Alcuin. Come in and try it.'

Alcuin was actually trembling with fear and looked like he might refuse.

'I will make sure you don't drown,' Galen said in a cajoling voice.

Alcuin took a reluctant step towards the water, crossing himself several times before he took the first step. As he did so, Galen stepped lower, forcing his friend to follow till the two of them were standing with water up to their armpits.

'You need to submerge yourselves,' Hatim said as he came bobbing alongside. 'Get the sweat out of your hair.'

Without warning, he placed a hand on Galen's head and pushed him under. It was only for a second and Galen stood back up, spluttering to find himself face to face with Hatim, roaring with laughter.

'Do it again,' Hatim said.

'Leave him alone,' Alcuin ground out from between clenched teeth.

'I will,' Hatim said, looking Alcuin up and down in amusement, 'so long as you too, take a dunking.'

Quick as a flash, Hatim pushed Alcuin under the water.

Galen grabbed onto Alcuin's arm and heaved him up, using all the strength at his disposal. Alcuin came up gasping for air and white-faced with shock.

'Don't!' Galen said, making a grab for Hatim's hand, as it looked like he was about to push Alcuin under again.

'But he is filthy and needs this bath more than we do.'

'Please.' Galen prayed Hatim would listen. 'We nearly drowned in the sea. It affected Alcuin badly.'

Alcuin in the meantime waded back to the shallows and crawled out of the pool, coughing up water.

'When your boat was shipwrecked?' Hatim asked.

'We were thrown overboard in the middle of a storm. Thankfully, we were washed ashore, but we were certain we'd drown and the terror from that time...' Galen stopped and shook his head.

Hatim gave him a considering look, then a shrug.

'I'm getting cold now, anyway. Let's move to the next room.'

Galen prayed the next room would be easier than the first two, as Alcuin gave him a hand to climb out of the pool. He had to make a grab for his towel halfway up as it was waterlogged, loose and threatening to fall down.

The third room had a tiled wall on one end and half a dozen narrow tables reminiscent of Hatim's operating table lined up on the other side.

'Now we lie down on the tables,' Hatim said, and the fat man and two other assistants who were completely bald emerged from a back room carrying towels, fibrous sponges and an armful of leafy twigs.

'What happens here?' Alcuin asked.

'Now we will get thoroughly scrubbed to remove all the dirt, then we will get washed down and finally we will be massaged with oil. Relax, the process is enjoyable.'

Since neither man could disagree for fear of what might happen to them, Galen and Alcuin dutifully lay down. Galen had been bathed so frequently he had an idea of what to expect. The roughness of the sponges didn't come as a shock, therefore, although the pressure the man exerted was greater. It felt as though all his skin would be scrubbed off his body.

Galen had lain down facing Alcuin and his friend's grimace told him that the experience wasn't a pleasant one for him either. But, aside from gritting his teeth and letting out a yelp of pain when he was rubbed too hard, he made no complaint.

Then the men took up the bundles of leafy twigs and slapped Galen's body from top to bottom, releasing a sharp herby scent as they crushed the leaves against his skin.

'For the love of God, what is this?' Alcuin's voice was heavy with misery. 'This feels only slightly less painful than when I was whipped for bad behaviour as a boy.'

'If this is the extent of the punishment you received as a child,' Hatim said, 'you were either spoiled or your punishments were exceedingly light.'

'Well, I was quite well behaved.'

'What about you, Brother Galen? I'm willing to bet you were very well behaved.'

It surprised Galen to be characterised in that way, but he supposed he had been a law-abiding child. 'I was very quiet. I rarely got noticed.'

'And so avoided punishment. I see.'

By the time the men finished scrubbing front and back, Galen felt like his skin was on fire. They were then all urged off the tables, lined up against the tile wall, and the bathhouse slaves threw buckets of water over them. Fortunately these were lukewarm and helped calm Galen's scrubbed skin. Alcuin looked similarly red. It was only Hatim, with his olive skin, that looked unaffected. Then again, he was used to this treatment.

Once they'd been washed down, it was back to the benches. Galen gritted his teeth in anticipation of what was to come and was surprised when the man standing beside his table poured oil onto his hands and rubbed them briskly together. An intense smell of frankincense assailed Galen's nostrils and then the bathhouse attendant rubbed the oil into Galen's skin. So that's why Hatim always smells like this, Galen thought.

Galen didn't enjoy being touched and the man's fingers were hard and dug into his muscles. He caused so much pain when the man reached his lower back that Galen had to clench his teeth to endure it but, all said, it was the least painful of the treatments so far. Alcuin, again, looked profoundly uncomfortable. Hatim, on the other hand, was so relaxed that he even seemed to drop into sleep if the light snoring coming from him was any sign.

Alcuin turned to look at him in surprise and then glanced at Galen and mouthed, 'Perhaps we can escape from here?'

Galen shook his head. The old men massaging them could incapacitate him without effort. Even if they got out of the bathhouse, the alarm would be raised within seconds and they had no idea where they were running to.

'We need a proper plan,' he whispered back.

How they were supposed to achieve that when they were separated and locked up was yet another challenge.

Hatim woke with a snort as the slave finished his massage and gave him a tap. He sat up, stretched, yawned and smacked his lips contentedly.

'So what do you think? Baths are good, aren't they?'

Galen wondered whether he was oblivious to how little he and Alcuin had enjoyed the baths, or was merely playing some sort of game with them.

'I can see how it is an enjoyable way to pass the time.' Galen weighed his words but also tried to understand why Hatim might like bathing.

'It's an excellent time for men to talk of the mundane and the sublime. Some of the best deals I have ever made were in the bathhouse. It is a great equaliser, you know, where no man has the trappings of power from his clothes, and the high can't be identified from the low.'

Galen doubted that was true. Maybe it was the case in a public bath, but not in the bath at the palace. There was also another pecking order with men's bodies. Hatim, with his height, handsome face and powerful build, could still lord it over smaller, scrawnier men.

Chapter 13

Galen woke not just because his constant pain always drove him from sleep but because he was hot. He supposed it was a sign of his improved health that the heat actually competed with the pain to wake him. After two months, he'd grown strong enough to sit effortlessly and walk unaided, albeit slowly.

Although he was careful not to reveal that fact. Galen worried that if he appeared too healthy, Hatim would no longer have an excuse to keep him in the surgery. He dreaded what might happen next.

Would he be flung into prison? If so, would it be with Alcuin and Bishop Sigburt or on his own? Once there, what would happen next? Would the amir tire of torturing the bishop and move onto him and Alcuin?

He wasn't sure if it was these terrifying thoughts or the heat that made him dab at his sweaty brow with the cuff of his shirt. He had to think about something else or he'd drive himself crazy. He'd never lived anywhere as hot as Halab. He'd even kicked his covers off during the night and his blanket lay strewn across the floor.

With a climate like this, Galen could understand why the Moors bathed at least once a week and more often if they were wealthy. Hatim had told him that further south, away from the cooling influence of the snow-capped Pyrenees, it was even hotter. Galen shuddered at the thought, considering how uncomfortable he found the current temperature.

Since the first bath, there had been four more at weekly intervals. Hatim had offered to make it more frequent but, despite it being the only time Galen saw Alcuin, he turned down the offer. While he had not actually grown to like bathing, he had become accustomed.

He'd also found that the cold pool, where they recovered from the heat of the steam room, supported his body and relieved his pain. It made the whole embarrassing bath experience worth it. The same was not true for Alcuin. He still hated it and Galen didn't want to distress his friend with more frequent visits.

Too many people watched and accompanied them to plan an escape anyway. But, since Alcuin had mentioned it, the thought of how they would get away preoccupied Galen's mind more than ever. Each time Hatim took him for a walk he tried to fix the placement of windows, doors and encircling walls in his memory. He hoped that one day this knowledge would come in useful.

In the meantime, he pushed himself to learn Arabic. At least one of them was going to have to speak the language if they got away. Although Galen had noticed that some slaves and more lowly visitors to the palace spoke a different tongue. It was reminiscent of Latin, but so changed it was mostly incomprehensible to Galen.

Hatim had told him, upon enquiry, that it was the local language, a melding of the local dialect and Latin that had evolved during and after the disappearance of the Romans. One language was challenge enough for Galen. But, if they were to remain prisoners forever, maybe he would eventually learn the other, too.

Galen shuddered at the thought. Luxurious as his surroundings were, he had no wish to remain in this caliphate. He couldn't be this far away from his family.

Aside from that, he'd never lived outside Christendom. Until his religion was ripped away and replaced by another, Galen hadn't realised how much his faith was a part of his identity and brought him comfort. Hatim might be right that they were all people of the book who worshiped the same God, but it didn't feel right to Galen. He missed the fraternal gathering of the monks and the unity of their belief, despite the disagreements, which were small in comparison to what he was facing now.

But that was enough musing. The call to prayer had sounded what felt like an age ago, which meant Hatim would arrive shortly for their morning class. So Galen eased himself off the bed, picked up the blanket, folded it and placed it beside his pillow. Then he took a walk to the fountain and back again until he heard the return of voices to the palace. Prayers were over.

Galen hurried back to the surgery and took out the coverless paper notebook Hatim had given him. It was half full now with the Arabic alphabet and a host of Arabic words written in both their alphabet and the Latin one, with the translations beside it. Lately, Galen had also copied in a few poems.

Hatim had recited one of his own, extolling the virtues of his horse, for which he obviously had a great fondness. Two poems by famous Arabic writers were added to this. Hatim had a similar book that was filling up with Englisc words and sayings. Although neither man had discussed it, they'd both avoided writings from their respective holy books.

All in all, though, since the Qur'an was being used to teach him the language, Galen had read most of the holy book. He was in general agreement with everything the prophet Mohammed had to say. It was on the finer points of theology that he disagreed.

Then again, he had a similar problem with the teachings ascribed to the Bible. He'd never said anything about that to anyone aside from Alcuin, who had been shocked. So the Qur'an would remain similarly uncriticised to everyone, especially Hatim.

Galen had just reached the end of his review of the previous day's work when Hatim arrived, this time only with his two male slave attendants.

'Good morning,' Hatim said and put down a bundle of papers. 'What do you make of that?'

Galen's face lit up as he saw what it was.

'That's Alcuin's work! You asked him to paint something for you.'

'As you suggested. What do you make of it?'

Galen lifted the first page and examined it, then flicked to a second and third and all the way to a sixth page, his face growing more and more amazed as he did.

'It's the story of our journey from Yarmwick to here.'

'Is it indeed? It seems that each image tells a tale, or at least it does if you know what happened. The first image is clearly the two of you working in a scriptorium, but the others aren't so obvious.'

'The next one is at my father's burh. That's my father and mother standing to either side of me,' Galen said, a smile of memory touching his lips.

'You get on well with your parents, do you?'

'Yes,' Galen said, looking thoughtful. 'I do now.'

'You make it sound like that wasn't always the case.'

'My father and I have a difficult relationship. My mother has always been my rock.'

'What of the next picture? That's obviously you, a group of vikings and a little girl.'

'Albreda, she and I hid away from the vikings, and then her mother looked after me because I...'

'You'd started to bleed. Alcuin told me about that and the way you forced him to leave you behind when the vikings were after you both.'

Galen flushed in embarrassment, which amused Hatim. Lately, Galen thought, Hatim was looking very pleased with him.

'You are absurdly modest, it's rather appealing,' Hatim said, confirming Galen's suspicion. 'The next picture makes no sense. I can see a king, crown and all, looking annoyed. You're in the middle of the picture with your back to the king and your right hand held out to a man who's on his knees with a sword in his hand and his face is blue.'

'That was at King Aethelred's great hall. Alcuin's father came at me... our family had a blood feud. But he fell before he reached me and my father intervened and agreed to pay the wergeld.'

Hatim seemed aware that he wasn't getting the full story, as his eyes narrowed suspiciously. Galen felt his face redden all the way to the tips of his ears and he hastily looked away.

'The next picture I understand,' Hatim said. 'You are being washed off your ship with rocks all around you.'

‘Yes.’

‘You were fortunate to survive that.’

‘We were.’

‘And the last one is you and Alcuin on the beach with the golden cross, surrounded by my uncle’s men. I recognise both him and myself.’

‘Your uncle is very distinctive with his dark skin and white beard.’

‘And your friend is an excellent artist. You were right when you told me that. I’m afraid I didn’t believe that he could do anything as good as my uncle’s artists, but he has produced something every bit as good as their best and a lot better than some.’

Galen smiled and felt as though he was being praised himself.

‘I didn’t believe Alcuin’s work could be so much better than the illuminated work I’d seen before either, but I was also wrong.’

‘So I am chastised.’ Galen barely suppressed a smile and Hatim sighed and said, ‘What have I said now?’

‘You are a very proud man. I can’t imagine you being chastised, not so easily, at any rate.’

‘And you are an irritating little monk to notice all these things and, worse, tell me about them.’

‘I’m sorry,’ Galen said, suddenly serious. ‘I shouldn’t do it.’

Hatim laughed. ‘And I should remember how quickly you back away from speaking your mind if I am too direct. Never mind, I will learn. Now here, drink this mint tea and honey and then you will eat your breakfast.’

‘What is it?’ Galen said, examining the plate that was filled with an unfamiliar grain, studded with what looked like white raisins. He'd only seen raisins once before. A ceramic container filled with tightly packed black raisins had been handed to his father with great ceremony. If memory served him correctly, none but his father had tasted what was, by all accounts, an intensely sweet delicacy.

'It's rice,' Hatim said. 'Cooked with saffron and sultanas.'

'Oh, I thought they were raisins.'

'They are dried white grapes. We give them a different name to the black ones.'

'And saffron?'

'Do they not grow the crocus in your land?'

Galen considered the question. 'It's a wildflower, common in our woodlands. I didn't realise you could eat it.'

'You can only eat the stamen, which is collected and dried. It is a laborious process and an entire field of flowers will yield only a handful of the stamen that provides a yellow dye used to flavour and colour food and for staining fabrics.'

'It sounds like the kind of thing only kings could afford.'

'That is true. And usually you wouldn't get anything like this, but there was some left over from my breakfast and as it has an interesting flavour, I thought you should try it.'

'You are very good to me, Hatim,' Galen said with a slight, embarrassed smile.

He didn't know how the Moor would take the compliment and it appeared neither did Hatim, for his face took on a vaguely shocked expression.

'I'm a healer. All I want is for my patient to get better,' Hatim said more brusquely than usual. 'Now eat up.'

Galen would have liked to continue the conversation but sensed that he'd discomforted Hatim to the point where he'd get snappy. It happened occasionally and Galen always wilted under any form of harshness. Instead, he turned his attention to the food, keeping his head down as he ate. Hatim settled on the opposite bench and flicked through his workbook. Galen glanced up once or twice, but Hatim was so absorbed he didn't look up once.

Rice, as with much that Galen had eaten here, had an unfamiliar but not disagreeable flavour. Since he'd never tasted saffron either, he had no idea what was rice flavour and what was saffron. The sultanas were plump, sugary little nuggets that he really liked.

He was less fond of the olive oil that the Moors seemed to add to all their meals. He preferred the fat in his food to come from animals, lard or butter, which the Moors didn't seem to use. Maybe the climate was too warm for that. All the same, he couldn't deny that the food was nutritious. He felt better, less fragile, and he suspected he'd actually gained some weight.

As soon as he'd eaten the last spoonful, Hatim, who'd appeared too sunk in his work to notice anything, gave the lie to that impression by snapping his book shut.

'Today,' he said as he stood up, 'I will do what I have promised for a while and that is to show you the library.'

An unexpected excitement flooded Galen's body. Since their long ago discussion about libraries, he'd been eager to see this one. But he'd held off asking about it for fear of offending Hatim. The man worked to his own timetable and acted on his own whims. Nothing Galen said would shift him.

'Since we are going into a more public area of the palace, you will have to be fully dressed,' Hatim said and one of his slaves stepped forward and held out a rust-coloured robe with a narrow band of light brown patterned embroidery around the neckline and the sleeves.

Galen stood to take the garment, but the slave shook it out, then bunched it up so that he could fit it over Galen's head. He wasn't used to being dressed by others, but Galen did what he could to make it easier for the man to get the robe properly fitted.

Hatim ran a critical eye over Galen, who noted his garb was more ornate than the slave's. Did this mean he had a higher status?

'Before we set off, how do you feel?'

'Fine,' Galen said as his eyes flicked briefly away.

'Are you in any pain?'

'A bit,' Galen said with a quick dip of his head. 'But it's nowhere as bad as when I left Lundenburh.'

'Perhaps we should wait a while longer, then.'

Galen looked uncertainly at Hatim and then his eyes flicked from him to the two slaves. 'They aren't going to help me walk, are they?'

'Will you need help with your walking?'

Galen wondered how fit he'd actually got with his morning walks and the wisdom of revealing it to Hatim. Since the only other longish walks Galen had undertaken were to the baths when he'd leaned on Alcuin.

'It might be wisest so that I don't do myself an injury. Maybe... maybe Alcuin could help.'

'Why Alcuin? Why not me?' Hatim said, and sounded more than just curious.

'Alcuin knows me, and he knows just how to walk so that I don't hurt myself. He... he has had to do it many times.'

Galen actually wanted Alcuin to see the library, and he wanted to see Alcuin. It might also give them an opportunity to learn more about their surroundings and possibly plot an escape.

'Not today,' Hatim said. 'Alright, let's go.'

Galen slid his feet into his slippers and hurried after Hatim, worrying about why Alcuin wasn't allowed to join them as the slaves took up the rear as usual, but closer to Galen lest he suddenly needed support.

Chapter 14

The route to the library was unfamiliar to Galen, so he paid particular attention to potential escape routes. Hatim and his entourage turned left in the courtyard and went via a much sturdier double door into an even grander courtyard dominated by a large rectangular pool. It reflected the three levels of columned balconies that rose around them and made everything seem even taller and more overwhelming.

'This is the part of the palace my uncle uses to conduct official affairs. It is in this building that he has his grand reception hall and the library.'

Galen nodded as he looked about, awed by the power of any man who could build such a magnificent palace.

'These columns,' Galen said, reaching out to touch one of a trio of simple white marble columns topped by a curvaceous pattern imitating leaves that held up the horseshoe-shaped arches, 'they look familiar.'

'They are Roman. Taken from their old buildings and temples to be used in the palace.'

'That would explain why they look different to the rest of your ornamentation.'

'But they are in harmony,' Hatim said and gave a brief nod to the eunuch Aleko, who was standing guard at another set of double doors.

Galen assumed Hatim's cousins must be in the room beyond if Aleko was around, and also gave him a nod of acknowledgement as he hurried forward, eager to see the library.

'Shoes,' Hatim said as they stepped inside and kicked off the slippers he was wearing, adding them to the collection already at the door.

That surprised Galen, but he noticed several carpets covered the floor like a colourful patchwork. The carpet nearest the door was a deep red with a blue and white pattern, the next overlapping carpet was mostly blue, white and mustard. He'd never seen anything like it. He stepped onto the carpet and his bare toes felt as though they were walking across a fluffy, short-cropped lawn.

'How strange.'

'What is it now?' Hatim said, but his face was glowing as it always did when he was aware he was showing off yet another superior feature of his civilisation.

'This carpet is wonderfully soft underfoot.'

'Ah, you don't have carpets in your kingdom?'

It was more a statement than a question. Since Hatim had travelled widely, he'd know about Christian homes.

'We have tapestries hung on our walls that are as beautiful as what you have on your floor, but we would never walk on them. They are too valuable for that.'

'It's why we remove our shoes. And we only do this in certain rooms, not everywhere. I would never put a rug down in my surgery, for instance.'

'Indeed.'

Galen's attention had drifted from the carpets to Jariya and A'isha, who each sat on a wide cushion with a low table between them. They'd been playing chess but were now watching him. Usually their gaze made Galen uncomfortable, but today a far greater wonder distracted him.

Shelves ran the length of the furthest wall and those shelves were filled with rows of books and cubby holes filled with tightly wrapped scrolls.

'Holy Mary, Mother of God,' Galen gasped.

'I knew you'd be impressed,' Hatim said with a broad smile.

'I've never seen anything to equal it.'

Galen was glued to the spot, stunned by the sight of so many books.

'Are you really going to give him access to all the books?' A'isha asked.

Galen blinked and looked at her. He'd understood her! After all the weeks of hard work, he'd actually understood what she was saying, not just gathered intent from her tone.

'He is a learned man,' Jariya said in her usual calm, level voice. 'Why shouldn't he read these books?'

Maybe it was because the conversation was about books that Galen could follow it. Then Hatim said something that was mostly incomprehensible but seemed to go along the lines of him doing exactly as he pleased. That would be about right for Hatim.

He had the same arrogance that Wilnoth, Galen's older brother, had. Although he'd died fighting the Vikings. It went to show that fate could intervene at any moment.

A'isha then said something of which Galen, mouthing the words as he listened, picked up only "uncle", and a general sense of disapproval.

'But, as Jariya said, he is a learned man,' Hatim said, giving Galen an amused glance.

'And a holy one,' Jariya added.

Her defence of him surprised Galen. Women, he'd found, were often kinder and more accepting of him. But if they had asked him to guess which sister might be more likely to support him, he'd have gone for the light-hearted one. Jariya had always seemed disapproving.

A'isha said something the tail end of which was, 'He doesn't look like a holy man to me. He's far too young.'

Hatim glanced at Galen again who realised Hatim had been watching him more closely than usual.

'Can you understand what we are talking about?'

'You said something about access to the books?'

'Quite right. I see all our hours spent in studying languages have not been wasted.'

'Apparently not,' Galen said, and looked hopefully from Hatim to the shelves of books.

'Go ahead,' Hatim said, and strolled along as Galen crossed the room.

'This shelf nearest the window contains our collection of Latin books. There are only thirty-two of them. Besides that, we have a half dozen in the Frankish tongue. The rest are all in Arabic.'

'What a wonder to behold,' Galen murmured as he ran his fingertips over the works.

Some were rough bound, coverless volumes, others bound in smooth leather. A few books had covers made from carved ivory.

'So white.'

'Elephant tusks,' Hatim said. 'Unlike your walrus tusk ivory, the tusks are larger and can therefore produce longer and wider sections for a cover.'

'I see. Have you ever seen an elephant?'

'A few times. They are impressive beasts, larger than anything you can imagine, with folds of brownish grey skin and enormous ears.'

'You have led such an interesting life.'

'I suppose you could say that.' Hatim ran his fingers along the books and pulled out two volumes. 'You are tired from your walk. Sit here and look at these.'

Galen was led to the closest table to him. It was like the low table being used by Jariya and A'isha. He realised that there were clusters of these tables and the cushions everyone used to sit on dotted all around the large room. How odd to have a room the size of a great hall dedicated entirely to books.

It was a long way down to sit on the floor and Galen wasn't convinced he could do it. Thankfully Hatim realised this and ordered his slaves to help. The men each took him by an arm and lowered him onto a cushion. It was the first time Galen had sat on one, even though they seemed to be the preferred choice of the Moors, that and just sitting on the carpet, which was what the slaves did once they let go of Galen.

Hatim placed the two books he'd taken off the shelf on the table and said, 'Tell me what they are.'

Galen picked up the first book and mouthed his way through the text on the cover.

'If I'm reading this correctly, it's a book on grammar by one Sa'id Al Baghdadi.'

'That's right,' Hatim said. 'You will find his work useful for understanding the finer points of Arabic grammar. You can take that book with you to the surgery and study it at your leisure. How about the other one?'

The cover of this book was made of ivory studded with gems. Clearly it was an important book to its owner. Galen had to open it to find the name of the author.

'Husayan isn Al-'Arif. This looks like a collection of poetry.'

'From one of our own, a son of Al-Andalus. He spent many years in Egypt studying but has finally returned to us and is now a teacher to the sons of Al-Mansur.'

'Is he a cleric?'

'Are clerics the only teachers in your land?'

'Not really. But monasteries and abbeys are where you find the most learned men. Although my first teacher was my mother, she taught me to read and write before I was sent to our priest for further education.'

'Ah, my experience was similar. My mother was also the one who taught me to read and write. I thought perhaps there were more restrictions upon women in your kingdom and few were literate.'

Galen found himself offended by the comment.

'Actually, some women are highly regarded. Our king's mother was the one who educated him and even now is in charge of her grandsons' education. She teaches them statecraft along with everything else.'

'So perhaps we are not so different after all,' Hatim said, and his gaze came to rest on Jariya and A'isha.

'Your cousins are also well educated, are they not? Jariya seems to spend her life writing things down.'

'She is very serious, that one. And their level of education is why I chose those two as potential wives. There are plenty of young women in the harem who know nothing about reading or writing. Some are beautiful and think that is all they will need, others excel at dancing or playing a musical instrument. But I want something more from a wife, especially my first wife.'

Chapter 15

'What are you doing?' the bishop asked as he opened one yellowing eye to watch Alcuin.

He was kneeling at the door frame, picking away at the wood by the lock and gathering each fragment into a little bowl that he usually used for his paints. Hatim had been pleased enough with his artwork that he'd ordered Alcuin to keep on drawing.

So most of the time he was working on an interlocking pattern of lions chasing deer, with their legs woven about each other and the lion's jaw fastened to the long neck of a stag. He was fascinated by the endlessly repeating patterns of this palace and wanted to show off the superior splendour of Anglo-Saxon knotwork.

But he'd also picked up on the rhythms of life in the palace and knew about the call to prayer. It was the time of day when his attempts to escape would be least likely to be noticed. So now he spent each prayer time scratching his way towards the lock.

He'd created a mixture of the wood fragments, mixed with shredded paper and some brown ink to form a cover over the excavated wood. He used it to hide what he was doing and was pleased when it dried into a hardened shape.

This he could push into place to hide his work and ease off to continue his excavation.

'Do you think you can escape?' Sigburt said, watching the activity.

Alcuin took a deep breath, stopped what he was doing, and turned to face the bishop. This was a conversation he'd wanted to put off.

'If I make an attempt, I won't be able to take you with me, Your Grace.'

'I am well aware of that, my boy. But you will take Galen, won't you?'

'Yes.' Alcuin worried about the defiance that came through in that one word. 'You want him to get to Rome, don't you?'

'I'd be angry if you failed to do so. Consider it a dying man's last request. You need feel no guilt about leaving me behind. I have spent sufficient time with the monster Zayd Al-Ifriqi to know that he is an implacable enemy to all Christians. He has no intention of letting any of us live.'

'Are you sure of that, Your Grace?'

'Oh yes. You and young Galen might not have paid much attention to the politics of the wider world, cloistered away as you were in the Abbey of Yarmwick. But I have observed the expansion of the caliphates of Islam with alarm. At first, they pretended not to mind about those with different religions. Indeed, some of our own brethren travelled to their capital city, Córdoba, to study the texts they have there.

'But their new khalifa, Al Mansur, is a zealot. He has held great bonfires of book burning, removing any Christian and Jewish books from their libraries. He razed the cathedral of Santiago de Compostela, one of our most holy sites. And he leads annual raids into the Christian kingdoms to the north, ensuring the kings remain weak and unable to rise up against him. And who do you think leads those raids?'

'Zayd Al-Ifriqi?'

'Ably assisted by his most powerful general, his nephew, Hatim Al-Qurtubi.'

'Mmm, I knew he was trouble,' Alcuin said and redoubled his efforts at digging through the door.

With a final push, a chunk of wood cracked off, exposing the sliding bolt of the lock within. Alcuin held his breath as he put his ear to the door. He couldn't hear a sound. Then again, if a guard was stationed at the door he was unlikely to be doing anything but standing, and that made no noise.

His fingers shaking from the combination of fear and exhaustion from pulling at the wood, Alcuin eased the door open a crack. All he could see was a fraction of the corridor. He pushed the door shut, shaking even more violently, and mashed his paste of fake wood over the lock, shaping it to look like the doorframe again.

'I'll leave tonight once everyone is asleep.'

At least Alcuin knew the bishop could keep his mouth shut even under the duress of torture. And he'd improved somewhat over the last two months since Zayd Al-Ifriqi had been away and Hatim had ignored him. But he'd not come back to full health, as his eyes showed, for they grew yellower by the day.

'I will pray for you,' Sigburt said as he pulled his blanket over himself, despite the heat, and rolled himself into a ball facing the wall and apparently went back to sleep.

Alcuin lay on the floor opposite the bishop and stared up at the ceiling. Ideally, he should sleep too. There would be none of that come evening. Only he was too anxious and excited to do so.

The plans he'd been making to get out played round and round in his head. First, he needed to get to Galen. That should be easy enough, as he'd walked to the surgery plenty of times now for the dreaded weekly bath and knew the route well.

Then he'd get Galen up and the two of them would have to flee to one of the gates. Alcuin had learned that there were four gates leading into and out of the palace. He'd decided the gates nearest the kitchen would be the best, as they were busy and a couple of men slipping out via the crowd were less likely to be noticed. Even his blond hair wouldn't look too strange as there were so many foreign slaves and especially as he'd landed up growing a beard. Both his and Galen's tonsures had also grown out, all a consequence of no longer having access to a razor.

The shadows of the bars on his window that Alcuin used as his guide for measuring the passing of time moved so slowly across the wall and ceiling it felt like time stood still. All the same, Alcuin waited and at least tried to force his body to rest even if his mind jumped over the what ifs of the journey.

He'd barely considered more than getting out of the palace and through the town. After that, he had no plans. Still, it was a risk worth taking, for he feared death was the most probable outcome if they remained. That conviction had grown stronger following his conversation with the bishop.

Time, despite the impression given, didn't stop. The room grew first bright yellow, then orange that was replaced by a bluish grey gloom and finally it was pitch black. Alcuin strained his ears to listen. Even in the dark there was plenty of activity and he waited till the sounds of voices gradually lessened.

All was silent save for the occasional call of an owl or the bark of some distant dog. Alcuin's nerves were humming now and he got up, unable to pretend he was resting any longer. Should he give it more time? Or should he leave now?

If he waited longer there was less chance of coming across a late-night straggler. But then he and Galen would also have less time to put any distance between them and the palace. He grinned in a humourless way at his assumption that they would actually get out. Well, there was no point in considering anything else.

Alcuin sat up and pulled on his cape. He checked the inner lining where he'd stashed what little food he'd been able to save in readiness for their escape, along with a few items they might use for trade: a pen, some gold leaf, paints and a paintbrush. Then he crossed to the bishop and gave the old man's shoulder a squeeze.

'I'm going now, Your Grace,' he whispered. 'Would you replace my mould on the door when I go? It might buy us some time.'

'Very well,' Sigburt said, 'Hold me up.'

Alcuin heaved the bishop onto his feet and guided the old man to the door. He listened for noises outside and then eased the door open. To his immense relief, the corridor was empty. Apparently, the locked door was considered sufficient security. That and the impression that their prisoners weren't that important. Alcuin supposed they were right. In the grand scheme for the caliphate of Al-Andalus, he and Galen were insignificant.

'I'll be off then,' Alcuin said, giving the bishop a nod.

'May God speed you on your way and keep you safe,' the bishop muttered, raising his hand and tracing a sign of the cross that Alcuin could barely make out in the dark.

'I will pray for you too,' Alcuin said and waited only until the door was closed again, then hurried, as quietly as he could, down the corridor to Galen in the surgery.

'Galen, Galen, get up!' somebody whispered and Galen felt fingers digging into his shoulder as he was shaken awake.

His eyes flew open, but it was a dark and moonless night and the hour disoriented him.

'Come on, man, if we're going to get away, we have to do it now!'

It was Alcuin! Alcuin was the one whispering so fiercely and shaking him in that controlled way intended to wake but without making a noise.

A shudder of dread shot through Galen, robbing him of breath and the ability to think. Then with a trembling hand he reached up for the painful grip Alcuin had on his shoulder and closed his suddenly cold and fear-numbed fingers about his friend's hand.

'Escape? Really?'

'I got out of my room. There's no going back now. If I'm captured they'll put me to death for sure. We have to go.'

'You would have a better chance of getting away without me.'

Galen's heart was banging against his chest so hard it was painful. He wanted to get away as desperately as Alcuin did, but he'd only slow his friend down.

'No!' Alcuin sounded more emphatic than Galen had ever heard. 'Not this time. If I have to throw you over my shoulders and carry you out, that's exactly what I'll do. Now stop arguing. Let's get out of here.'

Despite his better judgement, Galen tossed aside his blanket and stood up. The one advantage of the fear crackling through his body was the energy it gave him that meant he barely felt his usual pain.

'Let's take that.' Alcuin scooped up the blanket and wrapped it about Galen. 'It will make a decent cloak and it's a dark colour.'

That sent a pang through Galen. If he fled now he'd never again see the cloak his father had given him. He dismissed that thought as foolishly selfish when Alcuin was risking so much. He put on the slippers Hatim had given him, offered up a prayer to God for His support, and said, 'Let's go.'

'Good man.'

Alcuin took his arm in a grip so tight it made Galen wince as the two of them hurried out of the surgery and into the courtyard.

'Do you know where you are going?' Galen whispered as Alcuin dragged him across the courtyard.

'To the kitchen.'

'Oh yes, I see.'

Galen decided it was best not to speak. He needed all his breath just to keep up with Alcuin who was keeping to the deepest shadows and making sure he made no sound. Yet he was still moving quicker than Galen could do on his own.

They crossed the broad terrace that led to the bathhouse garden and Galen noted that only a few lights were still visible in the town below. They skirted the top end of the garden with its tall thin cypresses that stood like black fingers against the star-filled sky and made it to the kitchen without being seen.

'It's all quiet here, too. They must feel very safe to have so few guards,' Alcuin said as they skirted the plain, utilitarian kitchen block.

This was as far as either of them knew of the layout around the kitchen. It came as a considerable relief, therefore, as they rounded a corner and spotted the gates set into the castle walls. This turned into a shiver of fear because an entire platoon of men guarded the very solid, locked gates.

'What now?' Galen whispered. 'All the gates are bound to be the same.'

'I've considered this,' Alcuin said. 'It's also why I chose the kitchen for our escape. We can hide nearby and wait. If this place is anything like our king's great hall, the slaves will be up way before dawn to get things ready for the inhabitants. At that point, the gate will be opened and we can slip out when a big enough group goes through.'

'That is very risky,' Galen whispered.

'It's an escape. It was always going to be risky.'

'And entirely pointless,' another voice chimed in.

Light flared as lanterns were uncovered and Galen and Alcuin found themselves surrounded by heavily armed and ferocious warriors.

'Hatim,' Galen gasped and his legs went weak.

'Is this how you repay my kindness?' Hatim snapped.

'How?' Alcuin said, staring at Hatim as though he were a shocking ghost.

'Do you think we're fools just because we treated you well? Your guard noticed that there was something different about your door. One day, while you were at the baths, he discovered your secret. Since then, we've been watching you, day and night. I only let you go this far to see what you planned. I'm disappointed by this betrayal, especially from you, Galen.'

'Betrayal?' Alcuin shouted, his voice growing stronger even though it shook. 'How is it betrayal for prisoners to escape from their captors?'

'You are mine!' Hatim roared as his demeanour flicked from disgust to rage. 'We captured you. You are ours to do with as we wish. As a scribe and an artist, you have some value and I was hopeful I could convince my uncle to keep you for that reason. But now you've thrown that opportunity away. Now there will be no–'

A roar from the darkness cut off whatever Hatim was going to say as a horde of men emerged, running at Hatim, swords bared. At the head of this new group was a fat man staggering as he tried to keep up with the soldiers, but looking ferocious because of his height, bulk and his full suit of gold-edged armour.

Hatim actually tutted as he drew his own sword.

'Get them!' he shouted and charged at the heavily armoured fat man.

Alcuin grabbed hold of Galen's arm and dragged him backwards till they hit the wall of the kitchen.

'Maybe we still have a chance to get away while they're distracted.'

Galen shook his head. He'd had the same thought, but the gates into the town were still barred. While a handful of soldiers had run towards the melee, there were still sufficient to block any attempt to get through the gates. Besides, Hatim's men seemed to be the superior fighters, and the guards had also joined his side.

Hatim, too, outclassed the fat man that Galen realised was the uncle who wanted the governorship for himself. Hatim kept knocking him back each time the fat man charged him. It seemed he was toying with the man, keeping him occupied while his soldiers dealt with the attackers.

Galen wanted to look away. The roar of men in battle, the crash of steel against steel, the grunts and screams of the injured and the reek of blood and sweat held a horror that Galen felt could only be equalled in Hell. But even if he closed his eyes he couldn't remove himself from the battle.

He found himself praying that Hatim would win, even though he realised their tenuous friendship was at an end. Still, he suspected he and Alcuin would be better off with somebody who valued learning than with the indolent and greedy uncle.

In that, his prayers were answered. Hatim leaped forward and slammed the pommel of his sword into his uncle's temple. The man gave a surprised grunt and crumpled to the ground.

'Hold!' Hatim shouted, standing over his uncle's unconscious body. 'I'll grant mercy to anyone who returns to supporting me. There is only death for any traitor who remains with my uncle.'

It was an unusually generous offer that Galen hadn't expected. Few ealdormen would allow a man who had been willing to fight against them this way out of certain death. It seemed to surprise all the combatants, too, who stopped what they were doing.

The attackers looked uncertainly from their commander, flat on his back, to Hatim, looking remarkably calm, and then to the fighting men still standing. The uncle had recruited a larger number of halfway decent fighters, but Hatim's warriors were the terrifying Mamluks.

It only took one man to give a weary nod and drop to his knees, his sword held out in offering, to break the group. The rest dropped to their knees too and Hatim's men swiftly divested them of their weapons and rounded them up.

'To the training ground,' Hatim said, and looked over to where Alcuin and Galen were huddled against the wall. 'All of them.'

'I'm sorry,' Alcuin said as the two of them were prodded into motion. 'I didn't realise we were walking into a trap.'

'It isn't your fault.'

Galen clutched Alcuin's arm so tightly his fingers ached and he prayed to God to save them, for that was all they had left.

The sound of the battle had woken most of the inhabitants of the palace. Lights had flared in windows and groups of people flocked onto balconies and terraces to discover what the commotion was all about. Galen noted they kept their distance, afraid that to come too close might get them mistaken for enemies.

The defeated soldiers were led to the centre of the training ground where a hefty man stood before a chopping block with an axe by his side. It was larger than was necessary. Galen guessed that was for show and to instil extra terror.

'I will save your lives, but you will forfeit your sword hand,' Hatim said.

A wail went up from some of the traitorous soldiers, but not all. Galen guessed that even losing a hand was better than their life. The man with the axe then set about his grizzly task with alarming efficiency.

Galen shut his eyes, unable to bear watching such extreme punishment, although the dull thud, thud, thud of the axe could not be blocked, nor the cries of the men. But then it was done and the weeping men were led away, Galen prayed, to be treated.

'You,' Hatim said, a deep scowl etched across his face as he pointed to Alcuin. 'You're next.'

'No!' Galen cried, the horror of such an act too much to keep him quiet. 'Please Hatim, not his hand. He'll never be able to paint again if you take his hand. Take mine instead. The world will be no poorer for the loss of one more scribe.'

'Be quiet. What makes you think I will spare you, anyway?'

'Then take both my hands.' Galen fell to his knees, his hands outstretched, palms up. 'Please Hatim, take my life if you must but don't deprive the world of Alcuin's art, please.'

'Galen, no,' Alcuin said.

'Quiet!' Hatim glared at Galen, the scowl on his face growing deeper by the second. 'Damn you, why did you do this?'

'I just wanted to go home,' Galen whispered.

Hatim stepped over the body of his still unconscious uncle, grabbed Alcuin by the neck and pulled him away from Galen till he was standing in the circle of watching soldiers but, thankfully, some distance from the chopping block and its grizzly pile of hands.

'Strip.'

'What?'

Alcuin looked shocked and like he couldn't understand what he was being told to do.

'If you wish to preserve your hand and that of your friend, you will do as I order.'

Alcuin hastily pulled off his robe and stood, shivering and clad only in his underwear, in the torchlight.

'Flog him,' Hatim said and stepped away.

The axeman had apparently come prepared for all eventualities. He pulled a whip out from the back of his belt and set to beating Alcuin with such ferocity that every blow opened up a deep cut on his back. Galen stayed where he was on his knees and prayed with every fibre of his being for his and Alcuin's salvation.

It felt like the whipping would never end. Alcuin stood upright at first, but cried out in pain with each blow. Then he was knocked to his knees, and finally he keeled over and lay, unmoving and silent, on the ground, his blood dripping into the earth.

'Take them away,' Hatim said, and kicked his uncle, indicating he was also to be removed.

The guards evidently knew where they were supposed to go and dragged Alcuin, the uncle and Galen to an iron-barred door, then down a long staircase into the bowels of the earth where they flung Galen and Alcuin into one cell, and the uncle into another.

Chapter 16

It was pitch black in the cell so Galen couldn't see Alcuin. All he knew was that he was lying on the floor where the soldiers had dropped him.

'Alcuin? Alcuin, can you hear me?'

Galen shook what felt like Alcuin's arm but got no reply.

'Dear God, please don't let him die,' Galen prayed and felt along the arm, up to the shoulder, then Alcuin's neck, along his jawline till he came to his mouth.

He held a trembling finger under Alcuin's nostrils and waited. Was he breathing? It was hard to tell. In the end, after waiting, and wondering whether it was his imagination, he decided Alcuin was still breathing.

There was nothing he could do for him. He couldn't see his friend's injuries and even if he could, he had nothing with which to treat them. All he could do was pray and hope for a miracle.

Would God listen to his heartfelt pleas? If the sailors of the Wave Rider were to be believed, it was Galen's prayer that had brought down the lightning that sank one of the pursuing vikings' longboats. But aside from that one occasion, the miracles attributed to him appeared at God's whim and never when he prayed for them. Still, God had cured Albreda's misshapen knee and Uictred's broken ribs.

'It's nothing to You, please, God,' Galen whispered in the dark. 'Please save Alcuin. He wouldn't even be here if it wasn't for me. Please keep him safe.'

If God heard his prayers, he had no sign of it despite the hours, possibly even days, that passed. It felt like an eternity as Galen sat beside Alcuin's unresponsive body. During that time he grew dizzy and his mouth parched.

At some point the uncle woke with a loud groan and set to shouting and banging against the bars. Galen could understand some of what the man was bellowing but not all as he seemed to be rambling. He started out angry, demanding to be let out. As he was ignored and nobody came down into the darkness, he started pleading. Gradually even that died away to dry hacking tears and then just the occasional whimper.

Silence and loneliness swallowed them. This was a fearsome punishment indeed, Galen thought, as he cradled Alcuin's body and kept mouthing his prayers. This limbo of darkness with no promise of ever getting out was even more cruel than getting a hand chopped off. At least with that swift and brutal action the punishment was at an end.

'Galen?'

The word drifted into his silent world like a glowing ember rising from the fire.

'Alcuin! Alcuin, thank God, you're awake.'

'Where are we?'

'In a dungeon,' Galen said, scarcely able to speak because his mouth was so dry.

'Ah, this place.'

Perhaps the world started to move again with Alcuin's waking because before he could say more a loud clang came from above them. The sound of approaching feet and the flare of light. It was only a couple of torches carried by a pair of guards, but to Galen's eyes it was dazzling.

Hatim followed the guards but he didn't even glance in Galen's direction. Instead, he made for his uncle's cell. The man was so thoroughly chastised that he fell to his knees at his nephew's approach, clutched at the bars and begged for his life. Hatim looked unmoved and merely ordered his guards to haul his uncle out of his cell.

It turned into quite a battle as the man clung onto the bars and the soldiers battered at his fingers to make him let go, so he sank his teeth into the neck of one of the soldiers. But to no avail. The uncle was overwhelmed and dragged out and up the stairs.

Galen could do nothing but watch. He didn't even try to speak or attract Hatim's attention. It was clear the Moor was in no mood to forgive him. Bad as he felt, Galen couldn't bring himself to apologise either. He was a prisoner, after all, and would do what it took to escape.

'What do you think is going to happen to him?' Alcuin said, breaking into Galen's thoughts.

'I fear he will be crucified. I learned from Hatim that it is quite a common form of execution in these parts.'

'Ah.' Alcuin didn't bother to voice what they both suspected: that a similar fate awaited them. 'At least we're together this time.'

'How are you feeling?'

'Stiff, sore, dizzy, but altogether not as bad as I should be feeling.'

'There wasn't anything I could do for you.'

'Aside from offering both your hands?'

Even in the darkness, Galen could sense Alcuin's exasperation.

'It was all I could think of at the time.'

'Well, it probably saved both of us from that cutting block. I am thankful at least for that, and–'

What else he might be thankful for, Galen would never find out as the door to the dungeon swung open again. The screech of its hinges made Galen shudder and he held his breath at the return of the soldiers.

This time, Hatim stopped in front of their cell and glared down at Galen and Alcuin.

'Can you even stand up?'

Galen shook his head. His legs had long since gone numb as he'd knelt beside Alcuin, praying. The fear of once again confronting Hatim robbed him of whatever strength remained.

'There is still much I need to learn of your Englisc,' Hatim said.

'And I of your Arabic,' Galen said, wondering what the point of this exchange was. 'I'm sorry I disappointed you.'

'But not sorry about the rest?'

Even if it might save his and Alcuin's life, Galen couldn't bring himself to lie. He looked away from Hatim's fierce gaze as he shook his head.

'Ha!' The laugh was part angry, part exasperated and part amused. 'An inability to deceive is a serious handicap for any prisoner, or resident in a royal palace, come to that.'

Galen nodded, unsure what else he could say on the matter.

'Bring him,' Hatim said, tilting his chin at Galen.

The guards opened the cell and lifted Galen onto his feet, each man taking one of his arms. They hoisted Galen so high off the ground his feet barely touched it. It stretched his body, sending pain shooting through his belly and his legs as the blood went rushing back into them. Galen bit his tongue to make sure he didn't cry out. Then the guards marched after Hatim as he made his way back upstairs.

Galen might have submitted to this treatment without comment, but he worried about his friend.

'What of Alcuin?'

'He stays there,' Hatim said without bothering to look back. 'He will ensure your compliance.'

'Will you at least give him some water? Please, Hatim. And some light?'

'Who do you think you are?' Hatim spun round and brought his face so close to Galen's that their foreheads practically touched. 'Why would I listen to you?'

'I'm sorry,' Galen whispered, unable to hold Hatim's fierce gaze.

'My uncle will be back any day now,' Hatim said, and swung away again, stepping out into a daylight so bright it dazzled Galen.

What with that, and the dizzying spots of light in his vision brought on by pain and a lack of food and water, Galen thought it was as well he was being carried, for he could barely make out where he was, let alone walk.

Chapter 17

Within a couple of hours of Hatim taking Galen away, a slave was sent into the dungeon with food, water and Alcuin's clothes. They also left an oil lamp burning just out of reach on a ledge outside the cell, and the slave provided some basic treatment for Alcuin's wounds.

He was thankful that everything had scabbed over cleanly with no putrefaction and he'd not contracted a fever either. Alcuin ascribed his remarkable recovery to Galen. In his haze of pain, as he'd drifted in and out of consciousness, he'd been aware of Galen's hands on his arm, and the prayers he'd whispered hour after hour.

It wasn't a miracle. Alcuin wondered why not. Was he not worthy of God's blessing? Had he not looked after his own body and soul and those of his friend diligently enough?

Those bitter thoughts caught him up short. Who was he to question the will of God? It also gave him a chink of understanding into Galen's feelings. Was this lack of control over whether or not something happened what made Galen so wary of declaring himself a saint? And so anxious whenever somebody expected a miracle from him?

These thoughts now occupied his mind for a few days in the dim light of the dungeon. Looking after Bishop Sigburt used up the rest of his time. They had returned the old man to the cell a day or two after the appearance of the food and the light.

'Galen?' Sigburt had asked as they shoved him into the cell, a hunched over shadow of his former self.

'Hatim took him away. He said he still had much to learn.'

'So he is alive.'

'He is.'

'God still watches over him,' Sigburt said and curled up on the shelf-like bench.

He looked like a shapeless pile of shadowy rags these days. All his former arrogance and pride had deserted him.

'But God rarely prevents the execution of saints either,' Alcuin said, voicing his greatest fear.

'What will be, will be. God knows what is best.'

Sigburt's stoicism remained even after Zayd Al-Ifriqi returned to his palace and his interrogation of the bishop. Alcuin tried to do what he could to make the bishop comfortable at the end of each session of torture, but the old man pushed him away.

'You can do nothing to heal me. All you can do is prolong my agony. Honestly, Brother Alcuin, I pray every night for a release from my suffering. I believe I have earned my place in heaven by now, don't you?'

'Of course, Your Grace,' Alcuin said and held the bowl of water up to his lips. 'But at least drink something.'

That was all he could do for the old man and he obeyed his command to be left alone, even though the bishop was deteriorating before his eyes. Till one day a cry of intense pain woke him.

'Your Grace!' Alcuin scrambled to crouch beside Sigburt and put his hand on his forehead. 'You're burning up.'

'My arm, my arm feels as though it's on fire!' the bishop said in a whisper made harsh with pain.

'Let's take a look then.' Despite the old man's resistance, Alcuin pulled the bishop's arm out of the folds of his robe. 'Ah!' he cried as the cloth came away and a foul smell assailed his nostrils.

It was a smell he knew only too well and it boded ill. He pushed the sleeve back from the stump that had been left after they had chopped off his hand, so that he could see the flesh. The skin at the edge of the bandage was turning black.

'I have to get help.' Alcuin jumped to his feet and banged on the cell door.

It took several hours of banging to get a guard to come down to their level where Alcuin pulled the bishop to his feet and waved his putrefying arm in the guard's face. He retreated at speed. Alcuin prayed he'd left to fetch help.

He was surprised, though, when Hatim turned up. Alcuin decided against asking about Galen. He'd just assume he was alright for now.

'The guard tells me that rot has set in.'

To Alcuin's amazement Hatim had spoken in Englisc.

'I think so,' Alcuin said in Latin. 'The wound looks like it's gone bad. It's smelling something terrible.'

'Englisc, please. I have to practise this new tongue. Why wasn't I told before? For things to have got this bad, it must have been deteriorating for days.'

'Bishop Sigburt kept his stump tucked into his robes. He wouldn't let me see it.'

'Very well, I will see what I can do.'

Hatim waved for his slaves to bring their lanterns closer as he leaned in. His face wrinkled in distaste at the smell of decaying flesh when he bent down beside the bishop's makeshift bed.

'Tell me, where is the second treasure?'

The bishop opened pain-filled, bloodshot eyes and whispered, 'Really? Even now you would ask me that? I will never tell you!'

'Then I will remove some more of your arm, as my uncle has been doing.'

'Do you think I'm a fool? The arm has gone bad. If I am not to die, then you have to remove the rotten flesh.'

'Perhaps I should leave you as you are. See how long it takes before your whole body has putrefied.'

'I will be long dead before then and my secret with me. Do your worst!'

'Tcha!' Hatim said but also gave a shrug, as if it was the answer he'd been expecting.

Alcuin supposed he had to try. If nothing else, it would be useful information Hatim could relay to his uncle. Hatim then knelt down beside the bishop and cut away the bandage that had fused with the dried blood and pus.

'Ah!' Alcuin cried and staggered backwards as the bandage came away.

The level of decay was shocking. The flesh had melted away and the bone of the arm was standing proud of the black and green flesh and even it looked damaged. No wonder the bishop was sweating so profusely.

Hatim rapped out an order in Arabic and the slaves and soldiers who usually jumped to carry out his every command, backed away, some shaking their heads, their faces contorted in disgust.

'I will help,' Alcuin said and stepped forward.

Hatim gave him an impatient glance, then a nod, and turned back to examine the bishop's arm.

'It will have to be taken off at the elbow. It doesn't look like the rot has spread beyond that yet. Here, make him drink this first,' Hatim said and poured out a syrupy mixture into the bowl.

Alcuin recognised the look and smell of the syrup. It was the same poppy juice he used for Galen. It took more to coax it down the bishop's throat than it did for Galen to drink his medicine but it was downed quickly enough.

Hatim took out his knives and arranged them in size order while he apparently waited for the drug to take effect.

'You, hold him down by his shoulders.'

Alcuin nodded, knelt on the bench and pressed his full weight against the bishop.

Then Hatim gave another incomprehensible order and a guard went to the bishop's feet and also put his weight on the legs, keeping him still. Hatim had to be very severe with the guard who looked like he might pass out while he was holding the bishop down. He looked and sounded apologetic as he mumbled something in reply to Hatim's order, who just gave an unimpressed grunt as he bent to removing the arm.

It was bloody work, but at least the Moor was quick, and in no time he was sewing up the skin over the wound.

'You will have to watch the bishop closely,' Hatim said to Alcuin. 'He's going to need a lot of care if he's to live.'

'I will do my best. May I ask how Brother Galen is doing?'

'He's fine. His Arabic has progressed better than my Englisc. I've even got him explaining the meaning of your paintings to me in my own tongue.'

'That is good news.'

'Maybe. I would be interested to hear the stories behind the images.'

There seemed to be more behind Hatim's question than a mere request for the story behind a drawing, which worried Alcuin.

'All I can do is draw. You must ask Galen for the words.'

'I did. He told me the tale of some of what you drew but I got the impression it was not all of it. I've had a feeling from the start that the two of you aren't entirely what you lead everyone to think you are.'

Alcuin's eyebrow flickered briefly upwards as he gave a slight nod.

'I doubt there's a man alive who couldn't say the same.'

'I suppose that is true.' Hatim stood to go, then paused and looked back at Alcuin. 'It would be to yours and Galen's advantage if you tell me about the second treasure.'

'I've told you before, I have no idea what the second treasure might be.'

'But, in his current state, and if he grows delirious, your bishop might just give something away,' Hatim said with a meaningful glance. 'I won't hold your attempted escape against you anymore. Actually, I probably would try the same thing if our positions were reversed. But you are walking a fine line between salvation and execution.

'The fact that the two of you are a talented artist and scribe is an advantage. We can always use such skills. But you are also monks. If you refuse to renounce your religion and accept the truth as proclaimed by the Prophet Mohammed, I may not be able to save you.'

'Even if you get the second treasure?'

'It depends on what it is.'

'Galen thought it might be us, because we can produce many magnificent books with our skills.' Alcuin watched Hatim's face for a hint of how useful the information might be. He didn't even look surprised. 'Do you think that is possible?'

'If it is... I don't know,' Hatim said with a shrug. 'Perhaps if Galen is also a useful translator, it might help.'

'So you have forgiven him?'

Alcuin was relieved to hear that Galen wasn't only alive, but apparently Hatim was doing what he could to keep him that way. Although the Moor's less than enthusiastic expression gave him pause.

'See what you can do.'

Hatim's final words rang about the cells longer than the echoing footsteps and the shriek of the prison door.

Chapter 18

Galen wiped the back of his sleeve across his brow to mop up the sweat that beaded there and threatened to roll off the tip of his nose and onto his work. It had taken a while, four of the five months they had already spent in Al-Andalus, but Galen could now write from right to left with relative ease. He liked the hard-wearing reed pens and was also pleased with how his Arabic writing looked.

Linking all the letters together made him feel like he was drawing rather than writing, and it took some practice to get everything even. The loops above and below the main line of text also took some getting used to. His whole life, he'd worked hard to keep all his letters exactly the same size and perfectly spaced.

Still, when all was said and done, the final effect of the text he was copying was pleasing. It was an exercise from the grammar book Hatim had given him so many weeks ago when they'd been to the library. That had been a happier time.

There was a constraint between Galen and Hatim now. Neither man had spoken of the attempted escape again, but Hatim's cheerful air had become more brittle. His laugh was rare and sometimes forced, and he seemed less inclined to chat.

Galen, for his part, couldn't forget how he'd nearly taken his and Alcuin's hands, nor the flogging Alcuin had endured. Not to mention the horror of the days spent in the dark.

All the same, it felt like Hatim was trying to protect Galen in his own way. Galen was certain the demand to learn Englisc was a pretext to ensure Hatim could continue teaching him Arabic. Was it so important to be useful?

Galen had sensed from his earliest days that it was. For that reason, he pushed himself even harder to work from dawn to dusk, reading and writing at every available moment. After all, it wasn't only his life that depended upon his abilities, but Alcuin's too. That was more tangible than a second treasure whose existence he'd started to doubt.

The sound of footsteps came from the courtyard and, to Galen's surprise, Jariya appeared, trailed by Aleko. Galen had grown to like Jariya. He was certain she was also learning Englisc because she always appeared to be paying close attention when he taught Hatim. She also spent some of her time writing in her notebook during the lessons and Galen was sure it was in Englisc.

Aside from her interest in his mother tongue, she behaved towards Galen as though he was an equal, and worthy of her respect. A'isha was more dismissive and appeared to find it tedious to sit around during the language classes. Once she'd even started singing as Hatim attempted to explain a tricky vocabulary point. It had earned her a telling off from Hatim, but she'd won him round with a smile and a joke.

‘Can I ask a favour of you, Brother Galen?’ Jariya said in heavily accented Englisc as she sat down on the cushion Hatim usually used when they had their lessons.

‘Mistress Jariya, you have been learning,’ Galen said and felt a blush of pleasure cross his face.

‘I have been trying my best. It is an interesting challenge.’

‘So what can I do for you?’

‘You have many books in Arabic with which to practise my tongue. I have none in Englisc.’

‘That is true,’ Galen said. ‘But I have been working on translating the poetry of Husayan isn Al-Arif. It doesn’t have the same lyrical effect, but I hope it is still pleasing to the ear.’

‘I’m interested to hear it, but I was actually hoping I could borrow your book and copy out all the poems, riddles and translations you have in it so that I may have a reference work of my own.’

‘My book?’

Galen didn’t want to turn Jariya down, for he understood her enthusiasm. At the same time, he worried about losing his book.

‘If you would lend it to me each evening, I promise to return it every morning,’ Jariya said, as if reading his mind.

‘Oh, in that case, certainly.’

It reassured Galen that he’d see his book each day. It was bad enough to have lost his cape, but if his book also disappeared, he truly would feel adrift in this foreign land.

Just then, Hatim arrived and his eyebrows went up to see Jariya. She jumped to her feet, giving Hatim a slight smile but avoiding his gaze as she bowed and hurried away with Aleko.

'What did she want?' Hatim said in Englisc, following his cousin with his eyes as she disappeared through the main arch out of the courtyard.

Galen wondered whether Hatim knew how far Jariya had come in learning Englisc, and also whether it was a secret. Either way, he supposed it wasn't one he could keep since he was already in Hatim's bad books.

'Do you know she has also learned Englisc?'

'Has she?' Hatim looked surprised as he settled on the cushion Jariya had so recently occupied and his slaves took up position behind him.

Since he seemed uninterested in Jariya, Galen let the subject drop and waited for Hatim to get back to their usual lessons.

'I've brought you something,' Hatim said, waving at one of his slaves who placed a manuscript on the table by Galen.

'What is it?'

'Something you may find interesting. It's a codex of Arabic numbers by Maslama Al Majriti, another son of Al-Andalus,' Hatim said in Arabic.

'Oh numbers.' Galen switched to Arabic and hoped he didn't look too disappointed. 'I'm no good at numbers.'

'That's because you've only ever used Latin numerals. Let me show you our system. It's far simpler. You are clever. It won't take you long to discover how it works.'

Galen flushed with pleasure to be described as clever by Hatim and said, 'Very well, I'll try it.'

'You'll find it very practical, too, stuff you can use day to day. For instance, calculations merchants might have to make.'

Hatim's enthusiasm was so clear that Galen decided against pointing out that he wasn't a merchant and never would be. Then again, maybe this knowledge was one more thing Hatim was pressing on him to make Galen valuable enough to keep alive. So he turned his full attention to the numbers.

When Jariya returned with a tray of food for the men later in the day, the two of them were deep in discussion and Galen was actually stunned and excited as the ease of using the Arabic numbers became clear to him.

'This is so much easier than I ever thought possible. I've never liked the manipulation of numbers before and avoided them in favour of writing.'

'You see? That is the superiority of Moorish culture,' Hatim said.

'Yours is a very fine civilisation, there is no doubt. But I have very little to compare it with. All I have seen of the world is my home, Yarmwick, Lundenburh and here.'

'Believe me, you will never see anything to equal Al-Andalus.'

'Not even Rome? Surely there can be no finer city?'

'Rome! Pah, that is nothing. My uncle's town is very fine, but Córdoba is the finest in the world. The only city to compare with Córdoba is Constantinople, and even that doesn't quite measure up. It's old and crumbling, a shadow of its former glory.'

'How can you know?'

'Because I have been to both cities.'

'Really?' Galen said, his eyes growing wide in wonder.

'I studied medicine in Córdoba and I sailed to Constantinople a few years ago on a mission for my uncle.'

He was going to say more when Jariya returned. She looked put out that the food remained untouched and moved a pile of dates stuffed with almonds on Hatim's plate to where he was most likely to see it. Hatim waved her away impatiently. Galen watched her as she bowed and left the room.

'Have you decided who you will marry?'

'Now you sound like my uncle. He asks me that same question every day. It is wearying.'

'So you haven't.'

Hatim gave Galen an exasperated look and said, 'I'm leaning towards A'isha.'

'Oh.'

'Oh? You disapprove?'

'No, of course not.' Galen was overstepping his boundaries, but he couldn't stop himself, not when it was so important. 'Why A'isha?'

'She's younger and more biddable. I will have fewer difficulties with her. Jariya has a habit of looking disapprovingly at me and I can do without being nagged by my wife.'

Galen nodded and looked down at his food, fidgeting with the edge of a flat bread, wondering if he could say more.

'You disagree!' This discovery apparently fascinated Hatim. 'Allah only knows what business it is of yours.'

'It is no business of mine at all,' Galen said without looking up, and praying he wasn't making a great mistake.

'But you burn to tell me something, so alright, tell me.'

'It just seems to me... well, it seems to me that Jariya loves you while A'isha... she's prettier, but she doesn't think deeply and... and I don't believe she feels deeply either. Not for you, anyway.'

'So you think I should marry Jariya?'

'I would not presume to–'

'You already have. What makes you think Jariya cares for me? She's always more abrupt than A'isha.'

'I think she's trying to hide how much she feels for you so that she won't be mortified with shame if you don't choose her. But she does more for you than A'isha. She's more mindful of your needs and acts quickly to... to make sure you are never kept waiting for anything.'

'I hadn't noticed.'

'No. That was why... why I thought I might say something.'

Hatim laughed and shook his head at Galen, who was now squirming in his seat waiting to see whether he'd offended Hatim.

'I shall watch the two girls a little more and see whether I agree with your observations. But I warn you, ultimately the decision will be mine entirely.'

'Of course.'

Galen flicked Hatim a quick, shy look, relieved that he'd been able to say his piece. He hoped it might have some influence, but he doubted it would make any difference to Hatim's final decision.

Chapter 19

Alcuin looked over his meticulous counting off of the days, shook his head and counted again. He was not mistaken; they'd been captives of the Moors for six months. During those painful months the bishop had needed constant care. Now the old man was dying, although Hatim continued to send his decoctions for the bishop to drink. They provided temporary relief, but everyone, the bishop included, knew that his end was near.

Despite that, it wasn't the bishop who preoccupied Alcuin, it was Galen. Alcuin kept thinking back to the walks he'd taken with Galen and Hatim around the palace. It was magnificent, decorated in a riot of pattern and colour. If he wasn't a prisoner, he'd have found everything wonderful, to be marvelled at and stored in his memory to be used in manuscripts for years to come.

But he was a prisoner, he and Galen both, only Galen had seemed not to notice. Galen was so overwhelmed by the magnificence of the place he was letting his guard down. And worse, Galen was fond of Hatim.

As with anyone who showed Galen the least bit of regard, Hatim had won Galen over. He'd healed him, by all appearances better than Brother Benesing had managed.

He was teaching Galen Arabic and he was kind to him, all of which was fatal.

As Alcuin knew only too well, these were behaviours that Galen, with his confiding nature, couldn't resist. He had tried to warn Galen of the trap he was walking into, but Hatim's reaction had still shocked him when they were recaptured.

So how was he doing now? Now that Alcuin no longer saw him, was no longer taken to bathe with him or on the walks and no longer had snatches of hasty, secret conversations. Knowing his friend, Alcuin feared he'd gone back to liking and relying upon Hatim. It was bound to lead to disaster.

'Brother Alcuin,' Bishop Sigburt whispered.

'Yes, Your Grace, I'm here,' Alcuin said, shifting closer so that he could hear the man's voice.

'Alcuin, I'm dying.'

'We're trying our best to keep you here.'

'No... there is no point. I can feel my body failing... I did so want to make it to Rome but... now that's not to be.'

'Don't give up, Your Grace.'

'I have no choice, boy!' the bishop said with a momentary flash of his old irascibility. 'How can I prevent it? But I have your promise that you will go to Rome and tell the pope what happened to me, don't I?'

'Of course.'

Alcuin didn't bother reminding the bishop that he'd already made one attempt and failed. The old man's memory was fading with his health and there was no point in upsetting him.

'And Galen, what of him?'

'He is much improved. I no longer fear that he will die here.'

'Good... not that I am surprised. He has God's hand sheltering him.'

'Yes, Your Grace.'

Alcuin was inclined to agree after seeing Galen cheat death so many times. But he wondered whether even Galen's good fortune was running out.

'I would like very much... I would like it if I could see Galen one last time.'

'I'm not sure that is possible.'

'I am dying. See if our captors will grant me this one last wish.'

'Are you hoping for a miracle, Your Grace?'

'I wouldn't be human if I wasn't, huh?' Sigburt said, and his lips curled into a cynical smile that made him seem more like his old self.

'I will see what I can do.'

Alcuin was surprised and suspicious when the message he sent to Hatim via the man who brought the bishop's medicine got an immediate response. A quartet of men, accompanied by Hatim, appeared.

'We have come to carry Sigburt to Galen,' Hatim said.

Alcuin supposed it was necessary, for the bishop could no longer walk and his breathing had become laboured. He spent more time asleep than anything else. Perhaps that was why Zayd Al-Ifriqi had also given up on his torture.

'Come,' Hatim said once the bishop was out of the cell. 'You will have to keep an eye on him when he speaks to Galen.'

Alcuin nodded acceptance and hurried after the Moor. It was the middle of the day and he stepped out into hot, brilliant sunshine so intense that the packed earth of the training ground radiated heat back up at him as they trudged across. It was so uncomfortably hot it didn't surprise Alcuin there were no soldiers practising their drills. In fact, all seemed unusually quiet.

'What is the matter here? I have never been so hot in all my life!'

Hatim looked over the sweating Alcuin and said, 'Nothing's the matter. It is merely summer.'

'Summer? No, it feels hotter even than your damned bathhouse steam room. This is no mere summer heat.'

Hatim grinned and said, 'I assure you, monk, this is summer. Take my word for it. If you think this is bad, let me tell you it's far hotter further south than anything you are experiencing here.'

'Hotter! How can that be?'

'Someday maybe you'll find out. But for now, suffice to say that nobody stays out in the sun when it reaches its zenith here. To do so would kill you.'

That explained why Alcuin saw no people about and why it was so quiet. Even the birds were too overheated to sing.

'A heat so great it can kill you?' Alcuin said in amazement.

'It is the truth. You might gain some relief from the heat, however, if you removed that heavy woollen habit of yours.'

'I have nothing else to wear, and I shouldn't change into other clothes. I would be breaking a rule.'

'Galen is wearing something different.'

'You haven't given him a choice.'

'That also is true.'

At this point Alcuin realised they weren't going to the surgery as he'd assumed, but a different route that sent prickles of suspicion running over his skin. His misgivings grew when he and the bishop were taken to the room where he'd had his first conversation with Galen after his operation.

It was a strange, heavily shadowed room and despite the fact that it was noticeably cooler inside, it made no sense that they were here. Why not the surgery or even have Galen visit the bishop in his cell? Why go to the effort of carrying the bishop here?

They lay Sigburt on the ground in the centre of the room, in the place where they'd left Galen the previous time. Alcuin's eyes narrowed as he looked around, his vision adjusting to the gloom that was pierced only by the rays of light coming through the screen above. Then Galen walked into the room all by himself.

'Alcuin,' he said, with a relieved smile.

Alcuin was just as glad to see his friend, especially as he looked better than he'd ever seen him before. He still stood with a slight stoop, so he hadn't been relieved of all pain, but his face had more colour than it usually had.

'No guards?'

'They're waiting outside,' Galen said as his eyes flicked around the room and he took a hesitant step forward.

'Why?'

'What do you mean?'

'Why are they waiting outside? Usually we're both kept within sight of the guards.'

'I don't know. I recognise this place, though.'

'It's where we met before, too.'

'Oh yes,' Galen said vaguely and looked at the huddle of cloth in the centre of the room.

'Brother Galen, is that you?' the bishop whispered. His eyes flicked vaguely about the room till they came to rest on Galen and a frown creased his brow. 'Why are you dressed like our Lord Jesus?'

Galen looked down at his white tunic and pale brown overcoat and said, 'It's the clothing of the Moors, Your Grace.'

'Come closer boy, I have much I must say to you.'

'Of course,' Galen said and, with Alcuin's support, he eased himself onto his knees beside the bishop. 'What can I do for you, Your Grace?'

'You can hear my confession.'

'Me?' Galen's eyes flicked in alarm up to Alcuin. 'Surely Brother Alcuin would be–'

'No, it must be you,' Sigburt whispered. 'Will you hear my confession?'

'If it is what you wish, but... but I am not worthy.'

'You will do.'

Alcuin was less surprised by the request. If he was about to die, he'd prefer Galen as his confessor too. It had nothing to do with saintliness either. Alcuin knew Galen would accept all his sins without judgement, although that surely wasn't the bishop's reason.

'Very well,' Galen said and made the sign of the cross before bowing his head to listen.

Sigburt began his confession in little more than a whisper, but his voice grew gradually stronger as he spoke. It was clear that he intended to make a clean breast of his life.

Alcuin stood awkwardly to one side and scanned the room, wondering about its peculiar design, while he listened with half an ear to the bishop listing his sins. He had a lot to repent for. It seemed most of his life had revolved around plotting and scheming. That he still called himself a holy man after all he had done was a wonder. In reality, he sounded more like the lord of a vast estate than a holy man.

As the bishop came to an end Galen said, 'Give thanks to the Lord for He is good.'

'For His mercy endures forever.'

'I forgive you your sins and absolve you of all you have done.'

'Now, will you bless me?' Sigburt mumbled.

'What?' Galen said and jerked back in surprise.

'Bless me, Galen. Don't deny me this solace on my deathbed.'

'Of course, but I… I am not worthy to bless a bishop,' Galen said, leaning his head close to the bishop to whisper in his ear, his face reflecting his inner turmoil.

The bishop's lips curled into a smile.

'Poor, simple Galen, you are far more worthy than I to grant a blessing… Please, I am slipping away, don't delay.'

'Very well.' Galen looked deeply embarrassed as he placed his hand over the bishop's head. 'I bless you and pray for you. May you walk with God soon.'

The bishop sighed and said, 'I felt nothing.'

'What would you feel?'

'I'd hoped for a miracle. Well… never mind, obviously God wants me now and at least I go to Him knowing I never gave up the second treasure.'

'Why didn't you?' Galen said in an anguished voice. 'It would have saved you. You could have made it to Rome then.'

'None of us... are going to Rome. I fear what will happen to you and Alcuin once I am gone, but I never... I never gave them the second treasure.'

'No, you didn't. You were steadfast in your refusal.'

Sigburt laughed, a dry hacking sound which drained him of the last of his energy.

'My second treasure,' he said, his hand patting Galen's. 'My saint!' And with that, he gave a rattling sigh and breathed no more.

'Bishop Sigburt!' Galen said and gave the old man a shake.

'He's dead,' Alcuin said.

Galen took a deep, shuddering breath and gave a quick nod.

'Did you hear what he said?'

'I did. You'd do best not to repeat it,' Alcuin said as his eyes searched the room.

He was certain, now more than ever, that they weren't safe. A previously hidden door that blended into the lattice work of the walls swung open and Hatim stepped from a narrow hiding space, flanked by soldiers and looking unusually grim.

'Now we're in trouble,' Alcuin muttered under his breath as he moved to put himself between Galen and the approaching Moor.

'Hatim?' Galen's voice was hesitant, uncertain.

'My uncle wants a word with you,' Hatim said. 'Follow me.'

'The bishop... he died, Hatim.'

'It was expected. Now come,' Hatim said and pushed Alcuin out of the way.

Galen's eyes flashed across to Alcuin, wide with alarm. Alcuin saw the fear in them which reflected his own. He was certain that they'd been overheard, that this room was designed with eavesdropping in mind. What was going to happen now?

They'd worked so hard to keep the rumours about Galen being a saint from these Moors and the fool bishop had given it all away with his last breath. Not that it hadn't come as a shock to discover that Galen was the bishop's second treasure. It made Alcuin wonder what the old man's intentions had been for when he got Galen to Rome.

He shook his head. That didn't matter now. He had bigger problems and they all hinged on what was going to happen to Galen as the accompanying soldiers pushed him along in Hatim's wake. Galen was still a frail young man who struggled against pain every day. How was he going to deal with Zayd Al-Ifriqi knowing what the Moor had done to the bishop?

Galen felt as though he'd tipped headlong into a nightmare. Hatim's cold eyes bored right through him as he issued orders for Galen to be taken to the throne room. Then he turned his back on Galen. It was to be expected. He'd always known he was a prisoner, precariously balanced between relative safety and... what?

Were they going to torture him? Could he resist if they did? The thought of being tortured, of having his hand chopped off or worse, overwhelmed Galen. He felt sick and dizzy and the world pitched about him as he crashed to the floor.

'Galen!' Hatim said as the commotion from his men drew his attention. Galen was dazed and trying to push himself back onto his feet. 'Get him up!' Hatim roared at his men.

Alcuin hurried to be the first.

'I won't leave you alone,' he whispered as he pulled Galen to his feet. 'If we are to be tortured, at least we'll be together.'

Galen nodded as he struggled to regain control over himself and make his legs work.

'I was a fool. I'm sorry.'

Alcuin swore under his breath as he hurried Galen along faster than he could cope with.

'Don't think about that now.'

They were led into the largest room of the palace. Galen felt overwhelmed by the grandeur of the place that was designed to intimidate. A patchwork of fine rugs covered every inch of the floor and men poured in from every direction. It seemed like they'd been waiting for this moment.

Everyone kicked their shoes off as they entered. It was a strange detail to notice when so much was at stake. There was a growing pile of shoes added to the growing number of men who pushed their way in and then stood bunched together on either side of the room, whispering and pointing.

Galen shrank at the sight of all those strangers and he had to cling even more tightly to Alcuin to ensure he didn't collapse. To his horror, he realised that Alcuin, who'd always been so brave and who'd led him so confidently into the king's hall, was also shaking.

Zayd Al-Ifriqi waved his hands for silence, settled on his throne with the tall peacock tail backrest and looked over the crowd of men. His gaze lingered on his nephew's angry red face for a moment before continuing. The rest of the onlookers were a mix of highborn, well-dressed men, and soldiers. They displayed a range of emotions, some merely curious, the more bloodthirsty of them eager. It terrified Galen that they clearly wanted to see some brutal entertainment.

'Kneel,' Hatim said as Galen and Alcuin reached the midpoint of the room. Galen gave him a blank, scared look but didn't react. 'Kneel!' Hatim shouted, then stormed over to Galen and, with a crushing grip on his shoulder, forced him to the ground.

Galen gasped at the ferocity of it and subsided to his knees, sank his head and kept his eyes fixed on the floor. He couldn't look up. Alcuin cursed under his breath again. Galen realised it was his attempt to keep his emotions under control. Galen wished he could do the same as realisation hit him that Hatim was nothing but a stranger that he'd thought he knew.

Hatim stepped away and said to the guard, 'Don't let him get up.'

'So you are a saint,' Zayd Al-Ifriqi said, loudly enough for everyone to hear, his face reflecting his own amazement. 'That stupid old bishop allowed himself to be tortured over a small weak man because he believes you are a saint?'

Galen didn't move or speak.

'Silence won't save you, cur!' Zayd Al-Ifriqi bellowed. 'I know you can understand me, so you will answer. What makes you a saint, huh? Tell me that.'

'I am not a saint,' Galen whispered and wrapped his trembling arms around his body.

'Do you deny it? After your bishop said it was so? After he died rather than reveal this fact to me?'

'I... I have never claimed it.'

Galen's voice was barely audible. It was taking all his strength just to get the words out.

'Fetch the whip!'

'What are you going to do to him?' Hatim asked.

'That depends on how much of a saint he is. I'm not inclined to suffer a Christian saint to live, though.'

'So you're going to kill him? After all I did to get him better?'

'You got your entertainment from him and you've learned his language. What more do you want from him?' Zayd Al-Ifriqi said, as his eyes narrowed suspiciously.

'Nothing, of course. But why the whip?'

'Because I will test the so-called saintliness of this man. Saints are supposed to perform miracles, are they not?'

'Yes, so?'

'Let's see how well this one performs.'

Galen watched as Hatim clamped his jaw shut and turned his back on his uncle. Was he being tested, too? Turning his back on his uncle brought them face to face and Galen was shocked by Hatim's grim expression.

'I don't see how beating this frail young man to death is going to prove anything,' Hatim said, but without looking back at his uncle.

It hardly mattered what he said, Galen realised, as the heavyset torturer who'd chopped off all the rebel soldiers' hands arrived with his whip.

He bowed deeply to Zayd Al-Ifriqi.

'I am ready to obey, my lord.'

'Remove his clothes. They belong to me and I don't want them ruined,' Zayd Al-Ifriqi said.

Galen was so frightened that he barely registered anything as they pulled his clothes off him.

'Now, little saint,' Zayd Al-Ifriqi said, leaning forward to rest on elbow on a knee, 'tell me what makes you so special.'

'Nothing... nothing makes me special,' Galen said, his voice near to breaking with the strain.

'Beat him,' Zayd Al-Ifriqi said with a flick of his head to the man holding the whip.

The man took a deep breath, drew his arm back in a great dramatic gesture and swung forward with all his strength. Galen cried out at the sharp pain that ripped his skin. The force of the blow was such that he flew forward, unable to keep upright, and landed on his face.

He wanted to stay down, to curl up in his misery, but he couldn't. He had to show at least what dignity he could for Alcuin, his fellow Anglo-Saxons and Christendom. So he scrabbled to get back onto his knees and looked about for Alcuin but saw Hatim instead. He looked furious. Was Hatim angry because Galen couldn't withstand a mere beating?

The thoughts cut off abruptly as another blow cut through his skin and he lurched forward, a cry wrung from him.

'What are you doing, Uncle?' Hatim said. 'Why are you beating this defenceless little man? Just because some corrupt old man said he was a saint? For the love of Allah, he can't even keep the tears from his eyes. Actually, you would do better to threaten his friend.'

Galen gasped in shock at the suggestion and mouthed a no, that Hatim didn't see.

'What's that?' Zayd Al-Ifriqi said.

'Galen would do more to save Alcuin than he would to save himself. Don't you remember the beach? When you threatened to kill the sailors, it was this monk who spoke up and asked you not to. He was the one who told you where the first treasure was.'

'No, Hatim, please,' Galen said, turning to the Moor, 'don't hurt Alcuin.'

'You see, Uncle? Was I not right?' Hatim said and turned his back on Galen.

'I will tell you what you want to know.' A tear slipped from Galen's eye and traced the contours of his face. 'Just leave Alcuin alone.'

'So you admit you are a saint?' Zayd Al-Ifriqi said.

'I have never claimed it for... for myself, but... but others have said it of me.'

'Why?'

'It is... it is a long story.'

'I have all the time in the world.'

Galen barely managed a nod, or even to raise his head. The pain of his heart and his body was too great for him to hold himself upright as he slowly recounted all the things that had happened to him that made people believe he had miraculous powers.

'Is that all?' Zayd Al-Ifriqi said, looking far from impressed when Galen finished.

Galen gave a brief nod.

Zayd Al-Ifriqi sucked his teeth thoughtfully.

'I was expecting more. More from a second treasure and certainly more from a saint. What kind of saint allows themselves to be captured and tortured? Truly, you Christians have a trifling religion.

'If there weren't so many of you, you'd be laughable. But a hundred weaklings can always overwhelm one strong man, so it is best to be careful. Take him away!' Zayd Al-Ifriqi said as he waved his hand. 'He is boring me today. I need some time to think about what I do with him.'

Zayd Al-Ifriqi's words had such a chilling effect that it froze Galen to the spot. It was with a shock that he registered Alcuin take him so firmly by the arm that it hurt, hoist him to his feet and drag him out of the hall.

CHAPTER 20

Galen stumbled and Alcuin only just managed to prevent the two of them from falling as the guards pushed them both into the cell and slammed the door shut.

'Alcuin. Oh, Alcuin!' Galen cried as he held onto his friend.

'It's alright, I've got you,' Alcuin said as he half led, half carried Galen to the ledge of stone the bishop had so lately occupied. 'How is your back? I know the cuts of a whip hurt like you are being attacked by a multitude of elf arrows.'

Galen nodded, on the verge of a nervous collapse. Thankfully, Alcuin's matter-of-fact tone was having its usual calming effect. It helped stop the flow of tears as Galen fought to pull himself together again.

'Hatim did nothing.'

'He could hardly leap to your defence against his uncle,' Alcuin said as draped his long since discarded cape over Galen, being careful not to touch the wounds on his back.

'No, I suppose you're right. He couldn't defend us.'

'Although, I got the impression that Hatim wasn't as indifferent as I'd expected. There was a moment when he betrayed concern for you. And you know, in this place, with so many people in line to take over from his uncle, that was a major risk.

'His uncle was probably testing him, too. He might have wanted to see whether his nephew could distance himself from someone he's become fond of. He had to prove today that he could do what was necessary to rule when his uncle hands over his realm.'

Galen felt bad that even Hatim could be in a bind over the situation.

'I think... I think they're going to kill us,' he said and grabbed hold of Alcuin's arm with a trembling hand.

'Let's not worry about that till it happens, alright? And if it does, we'll die like martyrs, never recanting, never giving in to the godless.'

'I think I did that already,' Galen said, as his eyes filled with tears.

'You didn't deny God.'

'No, never that.'

'Then you haven't been broken by them. Don't worry.'

Galen crinkled into tears and hid his face so Alcuin couldn't see how desperately afraid and heartbroken he was. It had been such a blow the way Hatim had turned on him. He had no right to expect anything different, but Hatim had used his knowledge of Galen's affection for Alcuin against him and that felt like a betrayal.

Still, he had to harden his heart and prepare his mind for what was to come. Galen whispered a heartfelt prayer to God at the same time.

'Lord, I know I've been erratic with my vows and my behaviour, but I keep trying my best to be faithful to You. You know the plan You have for me, and I will try my best to face it with dignity. But please, please, Lord, don't let others suffer because of me.

'Please protect Alcuin. None of this is his fault. He wouldn't even be here if it wasn't for me. And if you could help Hatim as well. He is a healer at heart. I know he has done many cruel things, but I don't want to bring trouble to his door either.'

'What trouble?' Alcuin said from the dark.

'I didn't think you'd hear that.'

'It's a small cell.'

Galen nodded, even though he knew Alcuin couldn't see him.

'And don't go saying you'll protect me,' Alcuin said sounding grumpy. 'That's my job.'

To hear him being so protective actually brought a spark of joy to Galen's terrified heart. But as silence descended once more, fearful thoughts about the future abounded and kept multiplying.

At some point, he started getting delirious and was certain that the small lamp left burning outside their cell was multiplying, had started to hiss and was accompanied by bobbing black figures. Then he realised it wasn't a vision as one of the black blobs resolved into a familiar figure.

'Hatim!'

'Shhhh,' Hatim said, holding a warning finger up to his lips.

The other, smaller black figure proceeded to drip something over the hinge of the cell door.

'What are you doing here?' Galen whispered as he reached back to find Alcuin and give him a shake.

'What do you think?'

Hatim eased the key into the lock and with a click that sounded far too loud in the dungeon, opened the gate.

Alcuin came round at this moment, leaped off the bench and whispered, 'What do you want?'

'Seriously, the same question?' Hatim said, sounding exasperated. 'Why do you suppose I'd wander around here in the dark, whispering to you?'

The first possibility that leaped to Galen's mind was so desperately longed for that he scarcely dared voice it in case he was wrong.

'Have you come to help us escape?'

'You have?' Alcuin said, sounding dubious.

'Did you really think I would let you be executed?'

Hatim didn't wait for an answer, which was just as well.

'Not because you wanted to,' Galen said.

'I'm sorry, and in a way you have Jariya to thank for getting me to take action,' Hatim said, waving his hand at the second figure swathed in black.

'Oh!'

Galen had just assumed the second figure was one of Hatim's slaves. Now, she straightened up from crouching at the lower hinge and gave Galen a surprisingly bright smile.

'Jariya pointed out something I have known for a while, but have been in denial about. She said you are a truly good man. Somebody who makes us all better people for having you around. She then challenged me over what I would do for you.'

'Thank you, Mistress Jariya,' Galen said, deeply moved that this woman had spoken up for him.

‘That’s all well and good,’ Alcuin said, ‘but how are you going to do this? I mean, Galen doesn’t even have any clothes.’

‘Yes, he does.’ Jariya gave the door an experimental jiggle back and forth and the usual squeak sounded for only a second before the oil she’d poured over it worked its magic and the gate swung soundlessly open. Then she held out Galen’s habit and his shoes. ‘I also packed some food and drink for your journey.’

‘She’s quite a woman, isn’t she?’ Hatim said with a grin. ‘I’m going to marry her.’

‘You are?’

This further revelation surprised and delighted Galen.

‘You thought it was going to be A’isha, didn’t you? Well, I have to marry Jariya now, otherwise how will I buy her silence? Now hurry and get dressed. We don’t have a lot of time.’

‘How will we get past the guards?’ Alcuin asked.

‘I know many ways into and out of this palace and this city. Believe me, I can get you out. Whilst I am doing that, Jariya is going to drug all the guards on the more obvious route out of the palace. Once I get back from guiding you to the exit, I will open all the doors from this cell to the outside and then I will go back to bed. That way, when everyone wakes they will find an empty cell and every door standing open and they will believe that you performed a miracle and got away on your own.’

Alcuin grinned and said, ‘I like your plan. I pray it works.’

Galen smiled too, trying hard to hide how he was trembling with fright. ‘Thank you, Hatim, for everything.’

'Thank me once you're out. Now hurry and get dressed.'

Alcuin worked quickly to get Galen's old robes back onto him. It had been a long time since he'd worn them and the wool felt rough and scratchy against his skin and burned the wounds on his back. He said nothing about it, though. It would be churlish when everybody was working on an escape.

'What exactly are we going to do?' Alcuin asked as they set off up the stairs.

'There is a cart that carries the night soil from the palace to the fields to be used as fertiliser. Because of the stink, the guards seldom inspect it closely. They also expect to see it. You can slip onto the back of the cart after it picks up the last load.'

Alcuin nodded acceptance and looked down at Galen, who found himself giving a lopsided, half panicked grin.

'Well, I suppose it is a better plan than mine was,' Alcuin said, then shut his mouth as they'd reached the top of the stairs.

The guard who usually stood around the gate was slumped against the entrance. Apparently, Jariya had already drugged this one. Then there was a nerve-wracking long walk, skirting the edge of the training ground with only the light of a sickle moon to guide them.

'This is where Jariya will leave us,' Hatim said.

'Farewell, I hope you get home safely,' Jariya said.

'Thank you,' Galen said. 'I shall always remember your kindness.'

'But not mention me if you get caught,' Jariya said with a meaningful nod, and she hurried away before Galen could say more.

'Come on,' Hatim said and, much to Galen's surprise, took hold of his left arm. 'If we're to get to the cart in time, we have to pick up our speed.'

With that, he practically hoisted Galen clean off his feet and Alcuin had to hurry to keep up. Galen was amazed by the strength of the man and not only in how effortlessly he carried Galen while Alcuin huffed alongside. This close, Galen could feel the iron-hard muscle that was usually hidden under his silk robe.

The route Hatim took through the palace grounds was so tortuous Galen was sure he could never find his way back again if he had to. The last part of it involved inching past a guard, shuffling sideways along a tight, dark passage, and slipping into the plainest back courtyard Galen had seen in the palace.

'There, that's the cart,' Hatim said.

It wasn't necessary to point it out. The smell of human excrement that came off it was intense. The carter himself was a small man whose hunched over posture made him look old, even if they couldn't make out his face in the dark. He placed one set of buckets into the cart, and hoisted another, before disappearing back into the building.

'This is where I leave you,' Hatim whispered. 'Stay on the cart until it stops. Its route is to the fields on the eastern slope of the mountain. To the north of the piles of dung, you will find a narrow track. Follow this path till dawn. It will lead you into the Pyrenees and finally through them.

'Keep the highest snowy peaks to your right and stay in the valley. Don't go into the heights of the mountains for there is snow there even at this time of year and you can easily get lost. If you keep to the track, you should be in Christian lands in five to six days, where you will find plenty of people to show you the way home.

'This route isn't the most obvious one out of my uncle's lands and that will hopefully keep you safe. My uncle will be furious to see you've escaped and will be sure to come after you. If I can, and if my uncle doesn't suspect me of aiding your escape, I will lead my men down this path to try and recapture you. I suggest both for reasons of health and hiding, that you travel at night and rest during the day.'

'Yes, thank you,' Alcuin said.

'I have only one more thing to give you, over and above the food Jariya has provided.' Hatim handed over the sack he'd been carrying. 'Galen's books, and a vial of poppy juice for when the pain grows too great.'

'Thank you,' Alcuin said and clasped Hatim's hand. 'I don't know how I can ever repay you.'

'Keep a crusade from my door.'

'I misjudged you, I'm… I'm sorry,' Galen said.

'It took Jariya to make me act. I will never forgive myself for having allowed you to suffer the way you did.'

'I'll be alright. And without your surgery, I couldn't have fled this evening.'

'Try to take care. Everything will still be fragile. Don't push yourself too hard.'

Galen gave him a slight smile. They both knew they were in for a mad dash to get away from Hatim's uncle.

Hatim grabbed Galen in a firm hug and kissed both his cheeks.

'I wouldn't be so certain you aren't a saint.'

At this moment the carter reappeared and hoisted a final bucket onto the cart. He was about to pull the covering over the top when a soldier walked up to him.

'Damn,' Hatim said. 'We're in trouble if he intends to accompany the man to the gate. You wait here in the shadows. I'll create a distraction. The moment it's safe, head for the cart and get under the cover.'

'Alright.' Alcuin tightened his grip on Galen as he gauged the distance to the cart.

Hatim made swiftly to the other side of the courtyard, keeping to the shadows for most of it, but at the last minute he dashed across the far corner of the yard, his footsteps beating a loud staccato.

'You there, stop!' the guard shouted.

'Now!' Alcuin hissed, and dragged Galen to the cart.

The carter had followed a little way after the guard, then stopped briefly to watch what was going on. But since the guard vanished into the building, he gave a shrug.

Galen did what he could to get into the cart, or at least make it easy for Alcuin to push him inside. Then, ignoring the damp, stinking covering of the cart floor, he wriggled further in to make room. Alcuin only just slipped inside, pressed against Galen, when the old man returned and flicked the covering over his cart.

Galen prayed for all he was worth that Hatim's plan would work and that Hatim would escape the guard. He had more confidence in Hatim getting away than in them doing the same.

Now he tried not to think about what he was lying on and pulled his cloak over his face. It barely reduced the dreadful smell of human excrement around him. It was so intense his eyes burned.

The cart was slow and drips of sludgy excrement spilled out of the buckets onto Galen and Alcuin each time they went over a pothole, but finally, after what felt like hours, the cart came to a stop.

'Now!' Alcuin wiggled to the end of the cart, poked his head out, and then dropped to the ground. 'Quickly, before he gets here.' Alcuin grabbed hold of Galen with both hands and pulled him out of the cart whilst the carter grumbled at his mule.

Galen landed awkwardly, but Alcuin caught him halfway, hoisted him to his feet, and ran the two of them towards a great pile of festering dung standing proud of the gradually lightening sky.

'I didn't realise it was this late,' Alcuin gasped as they rounded the pile at the same moment as the carter got to the back of his vehicle and pulled the cover off. 'Come on, I see the path.'

Galen followed up the slope and pushed himself along, fear giving him strength. That and the need not to cause Alcuin any additional inconvenience on the journey.

'Looks like Hatim's plan worked,' Alcuin said as they reached a narrow, grey, rocky track.

'Yes indeed.'

Galen heaved a great sigh and regretted it as it filled his lungs with the surrounding miasmic air. He pushed that thought away because, towering above them, the peaks lit by the first early rays of dawn were breathtakingly high, snow-capped mountains.

'We need to keep that to our right,' Alcuin said. 'At least it's an easy landmark. And, as soon as we find a river, let's take a dip and get all this shit off us.'

'There was no miracle,' Galen said as he toiled along beside Alcuin, supported as he always was. 'God never intervened amongst the Moors.'

'Maybe he wasn't willing to reveal himself to a people who aren't true believers.'

'Even to save the bishop?'

Alcuin shrugged and said in a more cautious tone, 'Do you think he was worth saving?'

That was too dangerous a topic to pursue and not where Galen's mind was heading anyway. 'Maybe the miracles have stopped.'

'I wouldn't be so sure of that. Besides, it's pretty damn miraculous that Hatim, of all people, helped us get out. God is still watching over you, Galen.'

'He is watching over all of us.'

Galen felt a sense of relief fill his heart. They still had many challenges ahead of them, but he was hopeful they would eventually make it home.

Enjoyed this book?

Thank you for reading *Friend of My Enemy*. Your honest review will help future readers decide if they want to take a chance on a new-to-them author.

Get all my short stories for FREE!

Building a relationship with my readers is one of the great things about being a writer. Sign up for my no-spam newsletter that only goes out when there is a new book or freebie available, at: www.marinapacheco.me

Glossary

Al-Andalus: The Muslim-ruled regions of the Iberian Peninsula that ran from around 711 to 1492

Amir: a Muslim military commander or local governor.

Codex: a handwritten book.

Dar al-Islam: the realm of Islam. The Islamic equivalent to Christendom.

Ealdorman: nobility; this became the modern-day earl.

Enga-lond: the Anglo-Saxon name for England.

Englisc: the Anglo-Saxon word for English.

Eunuch: a man who has been castrated.

Habit: the clothes a monk wears, these consist of, a tunic (plain single piece robe), scapular a garment that hangs from the shoulders but has no arms, and a cowl/ hood, which is a long single piece garment with a hood and wide sleeves. It fitted over the top of the tunic and scapular.

Harem: a separate part of the muslim household reserved for wives, daughters, youngest children and female servants.

Lundenburh: the Anglo-Saxon name for London.

Mamluks: slave soldiers in service to muslim leaders.

Parchment: a stiff flat thin material usually made from goat or sheep skin and used for writing.

Qamisa: A wide-sleeved, long undershirt.
Saqaliba: a pagan Slav captured at a young age and castrated so he could become a guard for a harem.
Vellum: a high-quality parchment usually made from calfskin.

AUTHOR'S NOTES

Daily Life: As with all the Galen books I have tried to be historically accurate, but looking back that far is difficult and can always only be a guess. The clothes, food, and lifestyle in Al-Andalus are as close as my historical research permits.

Art: One question that may pop into your mind is the differences in Islamic art verses Anglo-Saxon art, particularly the representation of people and animals. In the early years of Islam there was less of a prohibition on representing animals and people. Even after religious art removed all such representations, secular art continued to draw people and animals. I have found quite a wide collection of images of life at court in Al-andalus.

Setting: This book is set in the fictitious town of Halab in Al-Andalus in the foothills of the Pyrenees Mountains near the kingdom of Navarre. Halab means white, and I used it as many of the buildings are whitewashed.

Riddles: The riddles and poems in the Galen books are my modestly reworked versions of actual Anglo-Saxon riddles. These riddles can be found in the Exeter Book kept at Exeter Cathedral. This codex is the largest known collection of Old English literature still in existence.

What's with the snails? You'll see a few snails in the book. They were quite a common motif in the page edges of medieval manuscripts, I suspect because of how slow it must have felt to copy out books day in and day out. I rather like them so I added them to this book.

ALSO BY

Get all my books here:

MEDIEVAL HISTORICAL FICTION ePub, paperback and hardback□

Fraternity of Brothers, *Life of Galen, Book 1* – Cast out for a crime committed against him, his future looks bleak. Until an unexpected visitor gives him hope for justice. A fight for acceptance, absolution and friendship in Anglo-Saxon England.

Comfort of Home, *Life of Galen, Book 2* – Proven innocent, he's returned from exile. Can he recover all that he lost? A tale of friendship and return to a family he thought he'd lost, set in Anglo-Saxon England.

Kindness of Strangers, *Life of Galen, Book 3* – Trapped in a land plagued by vikings, can one small miracle be all they need to survive? A tale of miracles, betrayal and friendship while under viking siege.

The King's Hall, *Life of Galen, Book 4* – As if

being commissioned to create a book to turn back the Apocalypse isn't enough, intrigue and romance threaten to destroy everything he's come to rely upon. Friendship, love and intrigue at the court of King Aethelred the Unready.

Restless Sea, *Life of Galen, Book 5* – Just when they thought they could go home, they're thrust into an adventure at sea. A journey that tests the bonds of friendship.

Friend of My Enemy, *Life of Galen, Book 6* – Captured by an implacable enemy, their future looks bleak. Will escape even be possible?

Road to Rome, *Life of Galen, Book 7* — A journey across a turbulent continent. Will Galen find the answers he seeks?

Eternal City, *Life of Galen, Book 8* — Galen and Alcuin delve into the secrets of the corrupt and decaying city of Medieval Rome.

AUDIOBOOKS narrated by Jacob Daniels

Fraternity of Brothers, *Life of Galen, Book 1*

Comfort of Home, *Life of Galen, Book 2*

Kindness of Strangers, *Life of Galen, Book 3*

The King's Hall, *Life of Galen, Book 4*

Restless Sea, *Life of Galen, Book 5*

HISTORICAL ROMANCE: ePub, paperback, hardback and audiobooks with AI narration□

Sanctuary, *a sweet Medieval mystery* – He needs shelter.

She wants a way out. Will his brave move to protect risk both their hearts? An optimistic tale of redemption with heart-warming characters and feel-good thrills.

The Duke's Heart, *a sweet Victorian romance* – His body may be weak, but his dreams know no bounds. Will she be the answer to his prayers? A disabled duke, a strong and determined woman and a slow-building relationship.

Duchess in Flight, *a swashbuckling romance* – She's on the run from a deadly enemy. He lives in the shadows of truth. When their lives merge, will their battle for survival lead to love? A reluctant hero, a woman and her children in distress, a chase to the death.

What the Pauper Did, *a body swap mystery romance* – How do you define yourself? Is it through your appearance, your memories or your soul? Intrigue, murder and romance in an alternate Lisbon of 1770.

CONTEMPORARY ROMANCE ePub, paperback, hardback and audiobooks with AI narration□

Scent of Love – Can two polar opposite perfumers overcome their differences and create a unique blend all of their own? Love, intrigue and clashing values in the perfume houses of Lisbon. □

Sky Therapy — A detective and the son of a serial killer. Is it safest to stay apart, or will they risk everything for love?

SCIENCE FICTION/ FANTASY ePub and paperback

City of Night, *Eternal City, Book 1* – World-threatening danger, a female demonologist, an unwitting apprentice, a city in a single tower, a satisfying ending.

SHORT STORIES: ePub, paperback, and AI narration□

Living, Loving, Longing, Lisbon, Vol 1 & Vol 2 – A collection of short stories inspired by the city of Lisbon, written by people from around the world who live in, visited or love Lisbon.□

Loves of Lisbon – An advent calendar of 24 short, sweet romances of the intertwining lives of the residents of Lisbon.□

FREEBIES: ePub and AI narration

Shorties – My shortest works: futuristic, contemporary and historical.

White Rabbit of Lisbon – A whimsical short story. What will happen when a rabbit and a raven fall in love?

Scourge of Demons – How would you deal with your demons? A short story set in the world of the Life of Galen series.

The Greek Gift – A Christmas short story. At the gym he

ignored her; will it be any different at the Christmas Eve party?

Christmas Fates – A Christmas short story. Aurora Dawn is about to learn the true meaning of Christmas and it has nothing to do with how many of the latest must-haves she can sell.

ABOUT AUTHOr

Marina Pacheco a binge writer of historical fiction, sweet romance, sci-fi and fantasy novels as well as short stories. She writes easy reading, feel-good novels that are perfect for a commute or to curl up with on a rainy day. She currently lives on the coast just outside Lisbon, after stints in London, Johannesburg, and Bangkok, which all sounds more glamorous than it actually was. Her ambition is to publish 100 books. This is taking considerably longer than she'd anticipated! □

You can find out more about Marina Pacheco's work, and download several freebies, on her website: https://marinapacheco.me □
Website: https://marinapacheco.me

Sign up to Marina's newsletter via her website or on Substack to keep up to date on all her writing activities, get early previews of covers and first chapters, short stories and freebies.□
Follow me on substack:
https://substack.com/@marinapacheco
email: hi@marinapacheco.me

Printed in Great Britain
by Amazon

61741466R00129